Teenage Hallucination

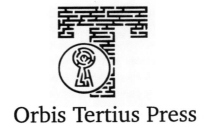

Orbis Tertius Press

Teenage Hallucination

Matthew Kinlin

Published by Orbis Tertius Press

ISBN: 978-1-7771304-3-5

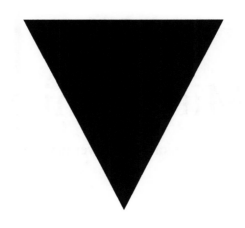

I

Mirror Thief

(a scorpion—thy silver throat)

"And Solomon inherited (the knowledge of) David. He said: "O mankind! We have been taught the language of birds, and on us have been bestowed all things. Indeed, this is evident bounty."

— Quran, 27:16

AIR

IRENE *(combing her hair)*: My hair is filled with money spiders and soft packets of insulin and fish oil. We were sold life insurance by the smiling man in a beautiful conservatory.

(Irene's blood rushes across the Atlantic towards children drinking cancer from blue and green cans of Sprite, ATM machines stacked with bad thoughts.)

BETTY: I am born from blue insomnia and locked in a suitcase.

FLIGHT ATTENDANT *(covered in snowstorms)*: Acting is reacting so when they say it, I just react.

BETTY: I looked down at Santa Claus wandering across hillsides into a pollution cult, limousines filled with Chanel werewolves.

(Enormous morning shatters on the windscreen. Betty points at a howling face.)

THE FACE: A moth decides to die in Los Angeles.

A hotel at dusk. A stranger begs to lucky colours that weep at the yellow exit. His body trembled before Malibu night. A receptionist and her mummified hands hover above the crocodile glyph—she speaks a name chosen and sealed upon his only body. And in a castle above the city, flowing through an exquisite hallway drugged with black poesies, his wives revealed the insignia of their adultery. Numerals etched into each breast dipped in red-black blood like a rune. Jealous silicone opens readily like purple fruit hung from sick trees, each implant living and engorged with Vegas pollution. Honduras servant in the kitchen mumbles fog. A suitcase buried in a trench —the twelfth wife (XII) drank gasoline and pushed her hand all the way through the skull past the sphenoid bone and leapt forwards through time and space into Mars—into astonished red sperm. She saw herself as an arrow, fountain torn apart into hot blood and bird shit. Their vertical billionaire descending upon his cockroach throne risen from the London parapet, saw Brazilians deafened in bright glow (IV)—white future light. A shadow makes its way across the wall, pornography paused and trembles. An apple tree hunched over in the car park—sunken, ten-headed imbecile. It prays for its own limbless springtime. Noon beginning to toll as an angel rises from its blonde hearse in a cloak sewn inside the bodies of wasps and bees.

O, to fall in love with a gorgeous bully.

The women open their arms to enzymes, each splatter of zoetrope blood, his repeating tangerine scream. The frothing toothpaste head passed around, and cable-tied testes burst into yolk. His pelvis bound in yellow, obedient ribbons like an Easter whore. The pale shape of an angel frozen across the wall. Impossible vampire, Nosferatu afraid at dawn. They saw a blue monster, each with mouths flung out— creatures drank in silver hair, mothers in white vinyl gloves. Appearing upon the table top as a Ouija mannequin daydreaming pink, dynamite throat torn into lilies infatuated. Its name was Metatron—pallbearers gobbled around the body. An orange coffin lifted into greedy clouds to meet the machine of bees—their only cannibal>>a yellow antichrist. His corpse sank into their blessings.

.

I DREAM A MONSTER

Chimeras drift through the garden like vaporous statues. They waltz across the lawn into slow wind—I enter cuckoo spit, the ghostly heads of lions. My father (a blackbird) sat beneath the winter morning as mother (a horse) climbed inside the Tethys Ocean expanding to fill the narrowness of her own thin bones, the diameter of everlasting sorrow. I lie amongst orange poverty and dine on orphic blobs, lobsters blotching true blue. I sneeze, float across the garden into dandelion stupidity, baffled homosexuals. The leering face of the television listens with a trumpet, its lacquered puppet head. We know the *death password*. We dance like suburban dervishes and walk on air—the D Ring, C Ring, B Ring. Ordinary goblins, we sit amongst constellations of dust that freeze to form a perfect circuit of silence: vase, lichen, a telescope plunged below Plutonian empire into cyan palace. A turquoise Orpheus swallowed beneath the bathroom sink, stalactites, nitrogen in his filmed cradle. We eat toilet scum burst into white cherries, vials of Nicole Kidman catalogue-poison stapled into her face and neck. MY BODY IS A RED ZOO, dogs on fire—a wolf spider running into the west, maddened lipstick.

I live in many webcam rooms: *the room of the staggering mirror, the room of the hunchback, the room of the crone.*

Through mirrors it came—gasped out of the television from an image as a fish that wanted to scream and breathe, fell from its own hated reflection like a wish. Light dashing across the purple screen in blazing spasms. A condom on fire, smell of cooked beef rising from blistered Qingdao wires. an eMBRYONIC bODY sMOKING uPON tHE mONITOR, iTS hELL cOCOON sPLUTTERED aND sTILL mOVING. The voltage of daily epiphanies broadcast from 444 Nebraskan spacecraft—a necklace crawled from its own silver-blue forehead & tongue, electrons rushed from the nearest reservoir. A river of salmon haloed in Toronto electricity and hurled from Saturn chamber.

It rose out of the sea, never forgiven.

.

7

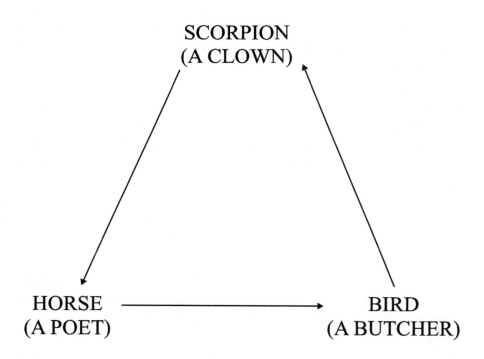

A television splatter of Alpha-Centauri-blasted, magenta UFOs descending above Gambian hostess as she drinks warm urine to overcome intestinal cancer, the hex of sea witches that swim and fuck hammerhead sharks.

To drink the blood of an angel is to go berserk and become a comet.

She yawned adrift in the luxury of shopping channels, a lake of blue-green brilliance. We watch stock markets on Neptune plummet into black magnetic gunk, a microwave open and filled with yellow sperm. Omni saints undress on a bed of pixels inside Bradford bedsit, unfold into pink asparagus. Oil painting of Virgin Mary on the computer screen fires parasitic ghosts into womb zone. $210,000 paid to eBay tyrant hidden inside his Yemen hovel—an eczema demon.

I stare into blank and empty screens, the widening face of a garden gnome. And we are blessed to travel to such new places, every toothbrush is now an airport. Trickling plexus as screen blissfully stretches upwards like a melting cat and we sit back in the summer of our own minds. We watch birds glide into urgent mist, sparrows engulfed in serene fire (X). A skull pops—opens—like a rat trap and locusts roar into sky flecked with feverish blood—glittering matrix of the dead. Taiwanese cemetery swimming in fireflies and red selfishness.

YouTube footage of Notre Dame burning to the ground. Paris evaporates into candyfloss. Gossip streams down our chins—an obese mess, strawberries on our famous lips. We are stunted, milkshake-idiots.

I walk across a silver lake in my transvestite gown—Marlene Dietrich upon the skinned flesh of squid and ermine, Medusa drank to death. A snake above a bowl of cooked heroin. Adam and Eve hide their inter-sex child in a grave of wands. Manchester turned upwards to forget the eyelash it abhors.

I have written the laws of paradise for it is mine to scorn and punish.

Corruption is always the beginning.

The mirror thief was born onto a sheet of glass —saw its own face coming towards itself (gobbling! gobbling!)—and it wanted everything. It moved through its mother's body like a rat eating through a wall. its hands appeared first as though it was climbing out of her—an intestinal monster, bones still soft and flexible, the expanding bubble gum skull: a Uranian King, a fly with 300 eyeballs. Shapes in her stomach coming out of her cunt like a poisoned kaleidoscope. She felt shit flowing too and pooling beneath the linen—chocolate filth for the poodles to fight over. Rhythm meant nothing as her bowels filled like blood-soaked balloons. she thought of the butcher's hands reaching among white kidneys, hacked and sprayed in orange fat—her own hands reaching up and struggling with the sun and the sperm that had fought its way inside her, the leaking puddle of glass—a son, seeing and alive.

The angel came out of a silver and crimson egg—a shell broken in plasma. My father (a butcher) had aligned five mirrors around the screaming tube and in the final mirror we glimpsed a reservoir of blood asleep upon the surface, the death animal = a white fox (a peacock-vampire). When a mirror reflects another horizon, it becomes giddy! and spins inside! and swallows THE FOURTH LIGHT IV.

An axis unable to die, surgical and sudden—a vertical slit from trachea to thorax. A ray of light that travels from the mirror—pierces an ashtray—expands into a seething bubble of mercury, the toxic blood of swordfish—their misery overflowed.

A dog buries itself alive in the garden & teleports into Sagittarius. A flickering grandmother in the corner of house waiting at dawn, her candle-filled mouth speaking of autumnal murder, the girl's body; pale and amber. An axe portal through the teenage-head-exploded into yellow acne. Butchered, a pointillist face motionless behind the glass like a detective in a bad dream, noir-nightmare stranger. Light can construct itself into many knives, folds its symmetrical limbs into a kind blade: a line into Los Angeles through limousine massacre filled with Chanel werewolves. The Holy Spirit rising from a champagne flute—wings tipped with motorcycle rubies, mouth crammed full with perfect oaths. Blood transfusions rushed into dying arms of iridium child heiress—$5 billion into Disney cocaine witch. Like a calf emerging from a sac of red stomachs, she opens her mouth into diamond smoke, a shimmer through B-movie fog, deaths gambled above her severed necks. The lonely sound of a piano in an amethyst Wes Craven fantasy waiting to never. *Midnight is purple and opposite.*

I//AM//THE//HEXAGON//BASTARD
BORN//IN//THE//MOUTH//OF//A//SWAN
IN//BLOOD//BENEATH//THE//CHERRY//TREE

.
.
.

My body is bathed in miserable Africa—I am a red scorpion moving through boiled corridors, snow macaques painted in families elated, voodooed shampoo. For I am the sin of treachery. I am the body of Judas Iscariot eaten alive on a bed of raspberries.

To see heaven through a shower cubicle, turned to face the masturbated glass, sorry like a butterfly—wings caked in tropical hair. Shit passed through the duchess keyhole, wife of colonial maniac—his own mangled slot rinsed in the saliva of slaves. A pair of Balmoral princes found guilty of incest—eaten into each other like buttercream, a mouth filled only with *more of itself.* ANNE BOLEYN STEEPED IN RED PHONE SEX PICKED UP THE RECEIVER and spoke of cannibalism as a map into endlessness—the green glutton forest. You shall be rewarded for each and every sin! I sit with schoolboys beneath vortices of flies that twist and speak into alien broadcasts from the Hercules Globular Cluster—crackling Lyra.

.

Our thoughts fast-forward into murderous cartoons, all synchronised beneath golden hair unfolding into Lisa Simpson—a wheel that smiles as the happiness floods in. We pull out eyelashes so we might resemble milk snakes, pierce an anus with a thumbtack to watch it wince in wonderful shock, the insides of grapefruits.

.

Through a webcam (3Y3BALL) we watch it remove red lice from the father dildo, swim into Lancastrian mirrors, a hilltop of the forgotten. When I reach for my cock, an afternoon expands into a yellow cobweb as the angel rises inside Ibizan smoke. In cherry red blazers we watch a clergy make love in Gethsemane as dusk begins to fall like snow—pink, enchanted upon the green castle. To become old and lie dying in conservatories among asters screaming and bizarre.

I kiss Christ again and again in the castle—lick.

Beloved vampire, our hepatic blood combined on a white handkerchief, Pontius Pilate on television as Dracula waiting in the keep. A bucket of cherub arms torn off like pork. Leather coal maze alongside skinless homosexuals, a human jaw torn off and glistening like pomegranate. Behold the light spilling and devoured through the attic. I lick shadows off the walls, *the liquorice sadness of the sun*. I love to eat the body of Christ (gobbling! gobbling!). I make my mouth large, an O. Around the shoulders and waist, I fit his entire flesh inside my mouth, MY LIPS ALL WET WITH CAR CRASHES.

.

Motorways burning as an angel rises in a coil of Ibizan smoke above the glass crucible that holds together the indefinite shape of tracksuits unzipped, an emaciated spirit—the perfect soul of Ptolemy appeared in piss, his cousins abducted from Jupiter and NGC 1300. Let us

14

drink his breath—crouched low to the ground, astronomers tied indigo and covered in frightened spiders. Lucifer rides out across Lancashire motorways as we see through watermelon storms like bored dragons. We gaze deeper into Blackburn rainbows; our chests are filled with banana fog.

We swim through valleys on an unending canal upon the back of a red and beautiful snake—our arms and legs stretch miles-long into *chewing gum.*

A sickle moon balanced on each unwashed cock end, our magic thoughts exchanged through serpentine, Mario glass. The expanded head of Bowser filling azure sky, the blue land of a sorcerer king. Boys invited into Liverpudlian's dungeon. A madman covered in Dalmatian panic. He shows them a glass cube, empty except for a single floating jewel. The death password = to eat emeralds in his silver hell. Locked inside a see-through fuck crate, daylight glowing inside the boy's torso, makes a trans-dimensional wish—trafficked marrow falling through bones into Europe below, inflatable Hamlet castle waving at children rushed into pineapple puberty. We, the sailors of the ship, tied the ends of Horatio to four horses (IV) and dragged him apart like a tortured dwarf. Green boreal sky rising as our throats fill with birds, unstoppable. Princess Peach swims towards us through a horizontal mirror, waters rippling and locked inside a wicked rainbow. She brings forth an invocation as we become airless inside crystal prison, her pink dream: Hesperus and Phosphorus, make thine eyes like stars (* *).

It should have been murder—with the rod inside her that twisted and saw her shame like a periscope but the child had crawled further and hidden behind her purple heart, scared and ticking like a bomb. It swam inside her pink brains—and there, finally, behind her own face, spoke with her mouth (mother! mother!). When she had danced with the master, she saw the crescent scar around his white member deflated into a lamb's teat, the left buttock cut off and stuffed with vulcanized rubber. His brass face leering through the toilet doorway—her legs strapped to the enema platform and jelly rubbed around her anus and mouth—apricot converse filled with silent, innocent seeds. Afterwards she commanded him to eat fecal botch from a silver bucket and laughed at his juvenile haste—a silver alien emerged in November treacle, the words coming from his own licking mouth now: mother, mother—another mouth inside the licking mouth, licking and speaking through homunculus teeth, a glass chandelier rising from her splitting chest, its head torn open like a blood-drenched egg. She saw a shadow fall away behind the mirror, crept somehow into the centre of the room. The creature was pretty and dressed in silver sex, a nightmare glorious of impatient sex—its feet bursting into blue flames, face covered in little folds like juniper berries, mouth opened into blue water. A flickering grandmother in the corner, speaking sadness into hand mirror: O death, where is thy sting? O grave, where is thy victory?

MIRROR I

A SCORPION ENTERS THE ROOM OF THE CRONE

A flickering grandmother drifts through the room. The doorway is thickened with cobwebs along the stained-glass corridor: purple and yellow light falling between wine glasses still laid upon the table, paused in the hands of skeletons and their never-ending futures. To say goodbye to summer each year, to watch it climb the lit window. She cursed the forgiveness of springtime that had welcomed the sun-SKULLS (X) back like a wartime hero, torso blasted in Milanese bathtub of blood and gunpowder. A soldier dressed in virgins, Italian and yellow besides the river. The crone lit a candle in the grotto and watched gondolas sink into liquid shit. We live in a haunted house. A vampire waits in lime green paradise, our dreams are internet-surfaced fangshi—a Hong Kong poltergeist gambling light across the table, the bartered princess waiting for Algerian dust.

In the sanatorium we are locked in red chains. Our mouths are filled with chairs that rush to fill an open shout. Furniture is disobedient. The warden sits in a glass tower dressed in silver dentistry, asleep among his exquisite machines that sing him into dreaming. The LOV3 MACHINE sealed in a glass cabinet. Its body is virginal cold and held out to him the murdered head—facial paralysis of an automaton. Sperm lived inside a golden cocoon filled with incapable hope. When the LOV3 MACHINE calls a name through the speaker, we move into the main hall, commanded to pray to an obscene mirror. A tin machine inherits this convex world. A blind girl shuffling forward. It ties her silver plaits to the Sussex platter and decapitates her, still outrageous—giggling. Newts decked in Assyrian gowns as the face injected with the notorious west. Here she smiles and the machine blinks, holds her in its programmed care. She had asked for nothing, born on a windowsill—had hit the glass like a fly pushed up to see daylight expand inside gigantic air. The sanatorium frantic and screaming as prisoners gather around the godlike mirror to look into ghosts they had conjured from themselves. A yellow phantom came forth and they knew its bones were glass.

We shatter like winter for its name is north: Metatron, the purple-winged bringer. The machine speaks from inside its diamond-littered cage: *the human mind is a palace of decay.* Lucifer chained to bed begins to laugh, pineal gland rising into moonlight like a purple iris—a blue harlequin.

Youth is hunger, sing the webcam schoolboys balding into birds—skeletal moss and filled with singing holes adored by the clergy. In blank classrooms we measured the circumference of our mouths, each traversed with glistening green protozoa heading north on vectors off the coasts of Bosaso and Djibouti: the tropics of gonorrhoea.

Our blood is clogged with spools of blonde—Hapi and Inset, carcinogenic reservoir solidifying over Cairo brothel, psychopomps stolen from Sala Ni Yalo (dead hopscotch).

In uncertain heaven (Murimuria) we gather around the hallowed image: a Spanish knight, Narcissus of Gerona afloat in a cloud of flies; his winged and beautiful children that ate the army of Philip II of Burgundy alive. We dress in October grease for we hear the beating heart of a dragon beneath our school. The mascara-clad eyelashes of Jesus Christ, a slut. His shattered Christmas blood ran down our backs and buttocks—risen once more and telekinetic. To see the world with the ecstasy of a surgeon! the geometry of a face reconfigured to the shape of His own demented mind!

We watch a torso melted into a delirious armchair, the convulsing ball of orange phlegm.

We urinated on a poster of a Catholic zombie covered in mining bees, ran into the spread legs of Californian fathers, lapping at slick vulvas. Our shadows tear from the soles of our feet for we are weightless and vampire, bodies of children summoned beneath pink Indian moon, levitating above wooden huts on tropical October plateau. Nightmares breathing in one blue cave. Scorpios forever.

.

To wank is to teleport into the bodies of total strangers. Maximum heartbeat of another in your chest like a magpie shuffling inside a shoebox—feeling the first desperate scramble, its simple desire for escape. The fear hiccups *back and forth* through his arms and legs as I stare at the bright Leonardo face, crayoned and squashed upon the ceiling.

A three-eyed teenage mutant ninja turtle.

I orgasm into glittering and atrophied muscles hung from buttocks like withered laundry—staring at the iPhone screen covered in babbling blue amphibians, their petty slobber.

Solemn pornography pauses around a blotching moon, magazines filled with mail-order sarcophagi, lesbian Korean confessions—her silver organs levitating above the fuck-stained nuzzle of rented Anubis. See cum ploughed into oyster silence, the wordlessness of her breath.

Another hyper-princeling tied and wanked in Madrid square surrounded by slender Chirico pillars tilting, toppled into fascism. I step through Manhattan 3Y3BALL (webcam) and reap dead souls from purple Styx, each wish swallowed down like a black orb. I live in a silent and purple underworld, a Manhattan apartment with drugged posies: *this is the room of the staggering mirror.* Nightmares breathing in one blue cave. We spread our ass cheeks in unison like Copacabana extravaganza—a blitz of yellow Easter feathers. October is the murder of July wires tightening around the malnourished twink fed into Poland. I rub sperm upon the sun. I betray daylight and halt before each cum shot in shuddering refusal. I deny the compulsion of stars. Escorts bred in the centre of a Vegas satchel, needle entering the sick and boiling neutron, a wizard expiring in a cloud of blood.

I watch a beautiful Pegasus run into a bus. I steal miracles. This noon has waited.

.

SUN = AUTHORITY

The sun and sperm had fought its way inside her and became gobbling light and then it was glass—spiteful and alive. The mirror thief could move through a wall or a plate of polished lead held up to its own blurred being—moved through itself, swam towards and into its own eternity. An atomic head open, then shut, covered in red ants like a zeppelin on fire. She nursed her son on bacon rind and powdered cream. It crawled around the basement of the master's house and screamed into cobwebbed alleys that led endlessly into nothing: purgatorial sewers, rat-running tunnels of blue cholera. It crawled across the bed at night and (gobbling! gobbling!) fed on her bones until she fainted in pain, tore open her upset blouse as it laughed and smashed the table top with its proto-fists (mine! mine!). It rubbed its penis and spat at her unwashed hands—ran through shadows faster than smoke. Her arms began to fade into dim-lit ash and a sunken skull stared back from the glass like her once flickering grandmother. She wept and locked the door but the child had crawled through the wood, screaming (screaming! screaming!)—and she recoiled in horror as its little head burst open like a jigsaw to show her a single flame beneath: blue then purple, a magician.

We read in books of the fourth magi that projected itself into the birthplace of Jesus Christ.

A reckless fool staggering through Mexican desert eating white anise and seeing red peyote numbers. An arithmetic of idiocy pouring from the blissful mountainside. He swims in warm avalanches. He drinks araq from a clay jug—pints of mint perfume poured onto the broken feet.

A clergy showed us diagrams of his battered head: silvery and blue like a Christmas bruise wiped with Texcoco cloth. Photograph of his time-travelled mistress, a blonde host jumping through a pale teal veil, Nietzschean azure unfurling on the fabric like seasickness, daylight imprisoned in the webcam. We gather around the angel, its graffitied hole spoken.

O death, where is thy sting? O grave, where is thy victory?

It climbs towards us from the corner with lipstick scribbled across hands as my red mother (a horse) turns to the rain-soaked windowpane. Horse demon with eyes of helium. Obese moonlight spilling through the desert valley—4s spinning in silent red darkness, egg spewing pink froth—we swallow into black and fecal rivers. We live in a haunted house where a piano plays a lonely song. The October slaves lower their heads inside haloes fed on Carolina mountains. The fourth magi wanders amongst wild pink flowers; his bounty of fruit to eat when the tomatillos begin to rot and dampen in flies. He now prefers to eat the flies to the fruit. The child-Christ does not disturb him in his cruel paradise and Earth continues on as ever. He sleeps beneath a waterfall and sees a throne and a staff made of flies. He is reborn with 300 eyeballs. He writes a final note in a journal. One becomes what one loves.

.

I am a scorpion and come from the west. Impregnated on a Los Angeles escalators, homosexual lore hijacked into green internet jargon. I unfold the plastic Sharon Tate transvestite face and speak a calendar month into the webcam. January made-to-eat fibreglass, wheeled out and tied to a desk chair. We watch its mouth fucked open with crypto-currencies like a screaming purple hyena.

The hands of Palestinians, lime green beneath evening sky— Chernobyl frogs that sing and transform into poison.

We pinprick the head of a yellow maniac for we are the extermination police and we like our bubble gum suits.

A pipe filled with cooked sperm. Rivulets of frosted glass melted in the mouths of pensioners. She watered incestuous plants and made a wish upon a brooch cleansed in water for 12 hours—uploaded images of a condom rolled down Japanese steel. Murder dreaming on a windowpane as she moved before the webcam, catching streetlight on her open chest.

Worried flesh watched in long corridors: her museum of shivering boys.

Undressed in the empty hallway. A hammer to the face! Bodies penetrated beneath pavements splattered with red leaves, his foot stripped clean in an apartment filled with fire ants. Brain continuing to sob from single fuck hole—cameras piled next to the talcumed corpse, his broken arms positioned upwards into explicit vogue. Loose, distended jaw, molecules flew from a spoiled, pampered skull faster than light—screamed towards the end of Kansas. A scarecrow without a brain still speaking into the microphone: *the body is an arrow.* Eating emeralds! the jealous heart of a plutonium witch! She reaches the watchtower of the clown, looks into Nebraska. She sees the Dorothy-corpse exploding into sunbeams.

Splinters.

.

MIRROR II

A SCORPION ENTERS THE ROOM OF THE STAGGERING MIRROR

The room of the staggering mirror found on a hallowed internet forum—cannibals that reach from their Minnesotan caves into sunlight swimming across torn and bloodied fingernails. They had heard of a computer swimming in the centre of the tenth sun-SKULL (X). Loud blue messages of tomorrow-clot born at noontime.

An apartment accessed through Facebook stream connected in Manhattan. The room is purple and ordinary. Dark walls with oak panelling, slightly peeled from the base. A blank television that reflects the empty mirror washed in pink Jupiter fog. A satellite spotted above Pennsylvania. Death planet sent beneath rainbow pyramid; a latter-day angel spewed from the eschatology channel 445.

Thoth curse recorded at Adam-ondi-Ahman, the child covered in salt and reading into camera. This body is a red zoo.

I teleport into alligators into red birds that tightrope across a guillotined Nazi wanked into face of Essex youth. A stillborn sun came out of its mouth through the television, its adopted sister— terrible opposite. A sapphire nailed to the forehead, Azure girls masturbate into dappling pink trays aboard a solar barge, beneath their Egyptian mogul covered in yellow lice. In the Cairo duplex, an 3Y3BALL spinning inside a cloud of blue dust, a methadone angel shivering on the bed surrounded by Persian motorbike goblins. To fuck a gorged and buttered face falling from the ceiling, to cackle an angel dying inside slow blue cancer. They undress in front of diagrams of a knowledge god eating through paper, madman applauding—Fox News necrophile dipped in gold. They tear off a boy-face and hold it to the light—pale and speaking into a mirror: *behold the currency of my love*. The rectum collapsed into red treasure. A new knave fucked and bloated in brine. They drink angel blood and see through time and space, apartments resurrecting like vertical spines on the end of a Russian peninsula. They witness Nicholas II of Russia transported into the future. Man made of silver water, Christian X of Denmark clone leaving seraphim chamber. It eats through their bodies like fortune glass. To glance over one's shoulder and see a reflection shudder—hold its breath. A mirror is the betrayal of itself, over & over again.

The mirror thief grew large and twisted through the doorframe—to glance upon its face and see poverty, rooms abandoned into solemn air, the monstrous shape of an afternoon risen above. She couldn't look upon it without falling (falling! falling!) as though backwards, down through her own dreams, a stairwell into the boiling kitchen with the maid and her blood-drenched pet. A lecherous terrier that gobbled (gobbling! gobbling!) and bit her tired feet, the sweat-striped legs sticky with exhaustion. The mirror thief had learned to walk into walls as simple as rivers: silver and widening around its flesh like an invisible apple eaten into the floor and resurfaced alongside a shimmering windowpane. Fog of bitten-breath close to the master as he withered upon his wooden throne, shat into an enamel hole. She watched as it danced upon the ceiling and crawled (crawling! crawling!) into the anus of the master into his open hollowed mouth, overflowing with oil-slicked flies and aluminium locusts—glass night formed around the lips into baffled shout, a shallow head spinning inside moonlit sleep, all his pretty blood frozen into silk. Six legs—a spider that hung from above and snapped off the neck. Death returns home.

It was the hexagon bastard with six legs. It was grotesqueness itself born in the mouth of a swan, mummified and hung from a bandaged tree—pulses washed beneath the purple Styx, feathers glowing in haemoglobin swill, ruby-red waste. To see a bird erupt from the carcass of a horse, its Nietzschean-doppelganger sent forward six months to rejoice again in Turin. Horse demon spilling with azure futures. The Himalayas reformed in sunken fire dimension.

To kill an emerald, one must whittle daylight into an arrow. Death wand carved from a single thread of Dorothy hair—her green head skewered like howling apple.

The hexagon bastard asleep in a bathtub of golden moths. Television spewing information through silent pipes—beloved pollution of a plastic Neptune. Our pornography-riddled and Californian graves videotaped. A Blambangan king cadaver sank into blue bumblebees multiplying.

Silver-green corpse spins and levitates above the television like a magic orb, six legs sprouted from orange torso—a web of skin stretched across the helpless face like a bloodied tambourine.

It is the spider king lost in Mesopotamian corridors of shattered money. Mark Wahlberg conquered by the Achaemenid Empire. Laris oculi, buccinators and zygomaticus torn off by space bacteria. A proclamation from a yazata orchid. Atar manifestation—orange shadows pouring from petals like greed, swans dragged backwards and gobbled (gobbling! gobbling!) into the speaking glass. The density of his carcass was always fire and we watched the ashen swan eaten inside its blue castle—game show hosts with their hands cupped with milk. An angel can only dream in television images. Blue and lilting skeleton. We are shown aristocrats and their slaves—a kind cyborg starved on an elegant satellite. The D3ATH MACHINE crying for freedom, eATS a hUMAN hEART.

mURDER tHE hOUSE

Night passing through webcam = glistening amphetamine, a coil of salt rising as a forest demon eats red pollen from crucible. My mother (a house) sleepwalks aboard a ship filled with mummified parrots, my father (a bird) is buried at the grave of an asteroid. I stare into Chicxulub crater below constellation of saints, blue and pink lullabies around obese Mesoamerican ghost—NGC 3242. A green temple appears on the computer screen; blonde hearse made of miraculous hair. Our coat of arms was a *dragon of ignorance* killed in a quadrant of orange-red rust. The plastic surgeon transformed into green fire. Insignia revealed his XII wives, arms rushing across the seance table to greet the deaf-mute brought back from her Hollywood coma. Hands trembling around a vase stolen from an Italian castle in a cursed valley—daughter wakes on Venice Beach and sees Yucatan Peninsula running with orange and silver blood of crocodile-Christ. Reptiles sat anxious on black eggs, the glyph beneath the receptionist's hand: green Venus. We wash our faces in dishwashers, cleansing salt. The demon stripped naked on a copper moon, cock and arse lubricated in cherry grease, pink face flogged beneath penniless sky—sold to the Azrael colony on Capri Chasma.

A schoolteacher once asked us to recite wonderful lies, a tongue of green fire above each teenage mouth. We liked to lick all lies and savoured each on our lips like summertime madness. We tell lies in July.

To lie is to become beautiful. I swallow the spit of a monster.

.

We murdered Saint Martin and digested his poverty into endless lakes of food.

$$$$$$$$$$

The currency of water-shit, amyl ether. We became sewage oligarchs.

A midnight toast raised to buildings! that feed on their own vertical children!

Our heads replaced with glass abattoirs, meat erupting into incensed and screaming birds. Yellow sun conures smashing into windowpane, a rainbow lorikeet drenched in hot and spoken brains.

We drink the sperm of a suited imp, his shining bowels washed and passed around. To fuck a gorged and buttered face falling from the ceiling—to cackle an angel dying inside a slow blue cancer. Its marbled arms dipped in heroin. Soft and pouting boy bruise, another head drilled apart like a godless pineapple. We eat bloodied carnations and orphan excrement plucked from silver piss, a mouth brimming with rats and cherries.

We are hyper princelings spread-eagled in an ivied hotel, our rectums fucked apart in wallpapered fright. We make our rectums large before the expanded webcam, like an O. We become pipes.

A friend willing to give his youth went to the river fishing—a flashing lamp inside his skull. Red algae ablaze in sunlight, petrol imported in heads of refugees ascending in the walls like illiterate wasps. I close my eyes like a flower praying into baffled moonlight. In the next room, a desert skeleton hid under a lampshade. It swills haemoglobin from the laminated veins of his painted gigolo, immortal in its see-through fuck crate. The slave reads their poem to the patient abattoir.

.

33

O obscene eye of the night,
    Let me see with silence
The darkness that is always soft and tender.

I undress before an old man and his dark
circumcision scar,
Touched on the leather of the tower by *envied
trees*.

A flashing (!) lamp inside his skull . . .
            His friend willing to give his youth
Went to the river fishing.

A hotel at sunset made him beg to lucky
colours,

            I close my eyes and enter your spit.

My skin is silver.

The mirror thief felt their own cold breath on the inside of the glass and looked out at the frozen wasteland—spinning snowstorm of dust and bloodthirsty heads, all decapitated (bleeding! Bleeding!) and hung from the ceiling on bobbing piano wire, jaws jumped (jumping! jumping!) as though speaking. Its own body trembling with violence, blue knives fell from its arms and mouth—a frightened scream coming from an empty black hole. To be born in East Antarctica, risen from the bottom of Vostok in a cloak of kerosene and ozone silence. The tavern had been filled with warm and amber men soaked in beer froth—the ginger tabby leaping across the fireplace: all stopped to see it enter the wall, mouth opening like a silver drawer filled with rusted nails. Cat arched and hissed madly at a gigantic shape spilling across the mantlepiece. Its hand reached out as a grown man burst into glass—all ghosts now, dancing in a fit of blue snow, the fire turned cold beneath its drinking mouth. All except one—an enemy of the master, in the corner alone and whispering (whispering! whispering!) into his cold skeleton hands: Lucifer alive in Antarctica. Laughter, an explosion of light as his mask slipped and cloak fell from deformed body—the village fool, a hunchback. Take my hand. O, child of night.

The angel descended upon the house in the form of fog. Its wings were Mesozoic foam thickened under four Laurasia sunsets. It spewed a golden oesophagus as tall as INDIA BLASTED INTO SPACE, DEBRIS-LITTERED FEET OF BLUE COMMANDO VISHNU. Digital Jaipur on a bedside, anagram of flesh crawling into Bhubaneswar dungeon. A boy resurrects in the hotel at midday covered in ochre flies—drinking, writhes in ecstasy beneath an ordinary crescent, the green shaking minaret erupting from his throat, casinos built on the Phi Phi wasteland. To speak the language of sunbirds released from a bamboo clap, his pimp dances beneath a tropical cum shot, boys gone summer and mad, awash in cheap Luppiter.

She (a horse) sees a ghost come to dance through the narrow streets of Jaffa—a HIV phantom conjured from the silent chapel. She watches a lamb cooked and crowned in silver moons. The tinfoil head circumcised into a spinning ball of blood. We are the wonderful gormless and stare blankly into clickbait: THE FOURTH LIGHT IV. To eat bubble gum from the floor risen with haggard magi dressed in Chinese fungi, their wart-ridden fingers. We lick helium ghosts that drag us inside gymnasts accelerated into chalk. To fold oneself away like clothing, and point at the sky—smoke typed into the melted screen.

.

SURRENDER DOROTHY

.

Noon is the smell of our favourite corpse and fluids we must pass through like electricity into gossip. We become shadows gambled on the wall behind the oblong entrance. I crawl through hibernating larvae to peer inside a keyhole and see an alien undress, ten skeletons, each holding a goblet of panacea. Rupert Murdoch descending upon a nectarine cloud, necro-animated arms dipped in black latex. A shuddering octopi applies makeup to a Vegas face, rubbing almond butter into the limp neck. The corpse of a quail torn open and giblets fed into the machine. A diagram of time travel nailed to a wall in a London bedsit—chimney head forced into colours. The glowing kaleidoscope of Piccadilly clots turned inside out, swivelled on the neck and about to burst. 698 names of Ornias scrawled in crayon across the walls of the house. It spoke of becoming the yellow antichrist—machine of bees, a vampire shape-shifted into a peacock, one blue-green 3Y3BALL. It wants to lick the blood of bees.

Sometimes at night I burst out laughing beneath injurious stars that begin to move and condense into a scream. The betrayal of Hamlet that beckons one closer into glass. Looked into the hand mirror of Ophelia into red-yellow-green. Her apocalypse is always slowness.

.

.

I no longer believe in human death, only the shattering of teeth—a pink skull exploded at noon, the vertex reversed into red shards glowing with cold and blind thought like silver eels. Coldness is my only religion. I count ten eyeballs extracted from the angel socket, tied to a desk—nerves torn like lightning from its cloudless back. We cut off a howling wing and hold it up to the light like a bloodstained shower curtain.

Silence draws its first breath like a closing portcullis—blue-faced babe smothered with a blanket.

A fluorescent yellow egg covered in scrambled fear: a Tamagotchi son. Its gnashing jaw opening like a horrible daffodil (gnashing! gnashing!). Their only cannibal, a baby born in October.

At the red end of the west there is only sand. The sun here is a blood clot on fire.

It lets out a scream. It writes a name in blood. The world has ended.

The hunchback held a blade of fire opal and led
them through a forest at the outskirts of the
village—forbidden to enter during the month of
October, a realm of wolves and seeing water ghosts.
The mirror thief shivered (shivering! shivering!)
under a cloak of the hunchback and saw the hump
covered in black ink, tattooed names of a boy loved
in winter. The moon was crashing (crashing!
crashing!) into a bruised sky as they ran to beat the
two suns, followed the map to avoid traps of faster
cannibals waiting in their meagre huts, their
worried children asleep in straw-filled cages. They
slaughtered a hen and toasted its bones away from
the path, stared into the flames and the mirror
thief saw the fire was glass. It approached the ice-
covered lake and walked along blue lightning
running beneath its feet—the hunchback trembled
to behold an anti-messiah dressed in holly and
birch, an owl covered in twilight. It showed the man
its own reflection in the water and dived into silver
hell, his face stitched onto a mannequin at dawn. It
sighed (sighing! sighing!) as the hunchback stood
pointed towards a blue castle on the mountainside,
his body killed & frozen into a weeping statue. The
hexagon bastard kissed his cheek and stole his kind
blade. It rose into the air.

A SCORPION ENTERS THE PALACE OF DECAY ON HOLLYWOOD BOULEVARD

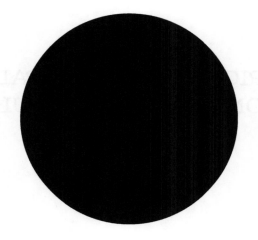

II

Eyeball Countess

(a horse—rivers run red)

"I could be bounded in a nutshell, and count myself a king of infinite space, were it not that I have bad dreams."
— *Hamlet, II. ii*

WATER

We become statues in a museum beneath our purple master. We switch thrones under its invisible hand for WE ARE THE KNIGHTS OF YOUNG SPERM, OUR RED BAZOOKAS.

Dead zero rising with Cup of Jamshid covered in mint.

We walk for miles in shoes torn from Devonshire marshland. When we reach the shoreline, our hearts grieve into purple-pink crystal. I weep into a pool of little eels that leap to taste the amethyst. Erect into foulest autumn, its forehead smeared in frozen dog rind—lemon torso climbed through the computer-skull to glimpse upon a pornographic face upturned. Bipedal Aaron Eckhart stumbled into grateful algorithms, dragged back through own sulcus and fired down the T1-T2 vertebrae like terror-stricken pinball gullet, silver-soiled pelvis.

I look into a webcam to come, hijacked and fisted inside entropic blue and white snow fallen in a Tokyo nightclub that welcomes the mikado and his beautiful parasite. An afternoon worm lived deep in the mikado's brain, dreamed only of motorways and leaves longer with English berries. She gobbles into the microphone from a glass coffin, the theatre of our shadows undressed in the zoetrope. We hold hands around members rubbed in calf fat, a tECHNO-pRAYER rISING tHROUGH bLUE aMPHETAMINE.

Look, she says—at all my little legs dancing. Do you like my hundredth toe?

We watch a chandelier split into vampires. Tokyo witches melted at a platinum factory (transmitted onto a haunted hill in 1609—asleep together inside new green skins). Each drains a sailor stopped to look into Shinjuku puddle. His watery face once thrown from a Derbyshire terrace. A curtain pulled back to reveal goose quill frenzied to see the boy return from vermilion gonorrhoea. To rise from his damp bed and look into THE FOURTH LIGHT IV bordered on newest locusts programmed to burst into gasping fire. A voice in the mutant back.

Do you enjoy the freckles and the shoulders they feed upon? Do you like the shape of my mouth when the ghost begins to sing?

.

We know the mistakes that thieves always make: too hot-headed and shouting at a cashier that looks just like his daddy-cop killed with a steady Time Crisis aim, shocked at the perfect kill—aorta flapping like red liquorice, muscles recoiling in stunned pleasure.

A nuclear explosion, cattle dissolve into hissing and scrambled shapes.

.

The waitress smiles with plain green eyes. Ozma in the deserted city.

.

Holes fingered into cardboard vendors and undead genitals. Madagascar still alive inside an aerosol can. From Blackpool pier we yell through flashing fog at forgotten planets circling the sun-SKULLS (X), at the carelessness of Pluto and Saturn, at kitchen utensils.

A leather sorceress sells dolls from a shopping cart and vials of human plasma.

We urinate on the poster of an iridium billionaire—his Yukata face covered in mining bees. We take turns to scream in hope somehow a creature might fly out: black velvet, a Herzog bat.

44

Images on the television of the Amazon rainforest on fire, a conquistador levitating above wooden huts, married his daughter inside lice paradise, hands covered in blinking orange malaria. *October emerges.* The weightless bodies of children rising beneath pink tropical moons, metabolic sleep-sickness. Scorpios feasted on opium and glowing banana fronds—maddened upon the October eclipse plateau, nightmares breathing in one blue cave. We drink morphine from polystyrene cups and wait in internet cafes covered in red blood cells. Our mouths are illuminated only with white fingernails combusting, bruised and smeared in acetone polish. Zombies smothered in isotopes die in Brazilian hotels. Our one thousand organs are balconies.

YOUTH IS HUNGER

·

My father (a flamingo) waits inside the attic for an echo from the Sala Ni Yalo (souls sank into black Venice), its glass-lined lagoons stacked with cages of shattered doves, their bright and obscene, turquoise droppings.

Daylight crawls through the ceiling into the house like boredom and fills an empty bottle, perfect in its exact measure. A spider watching murder dreamed on the windowpane.

My mother flowing and connected to another head taped to the bathroom faucet, green pipes routed into VAL3NTIN3 COFFIN sealed and entombed with dishwasher tablets. She has learned of the LOV3 MACHINE built by deaf Taiwanese robots straddled in unison.

The true name of *Luppiter* whispered from a latex-sealed mouth. Crocodile glyph painted on in Kyoto. Nangganangga carried on a ship into luxury abattoir, scales coated in pigeon fat. She feels safe in Bethlehem among buckets kept at her feet and flung forward from Mesopotamia. JOHN THE BAPTIZER.

She opens the dishwasher at noon into a flock of canaries and reads the labels translated from Mandarin: instructions into Gondwana—a bright blue fissure beneath the Indian Ocean. She sees oilbirds adrift in glorious steam as she leans down to scoop the broken head sodden inside the machine: tHE bAPTIZER cYBORG, wires trailing from its Xi'an larynx (thy silver throat) still spitting green acid. A toothpaste head passed round.

King Herod, porcine and laughs above boy slaves doodled in kohl, legs chained to a glamourous vulture, feathers emaciated and dressed in a topaz corset.

She cherishes detergent like sand because it is faster than water.

.

歌曲之歌

1. Builders (to clean and get rid of the water hardness).

2. Bleaches (to tackle bleachable stains).

3. Enzymes (to break down starch and protein-based foods).

4. Surfactants (to brighten glass).

5. Auxiliary ingredients (to break down the tablets and ensure all activities dissolve into the wash).

.

The servant boy hadn't meant to look (looking! looking!) at the silverware reflected from the cabinet. So bright and clean as her many faces spread out like headless queens glistening in the broken evening light. A tadpole staring through a red egg at cold, sleeping water. He had once seen scalpels led on a table coated with green and eternal soaps—and a chisel to break apart a skull. He began to weep and then shook (shaking! shaking!) with fear as she appeared on the back of a zebra, hands cradled in Chinese wolf spider. She made him watch her pull out the heart like a plum and examine its secrecy, animal whinnying into night air from the window of her far side palace. Eyeballs spread across her blinking nose and forehead—a red and silver puddle drinking (drinking! drinking!) through and crawled from the darkened chapel—shadows that reached (reaching! reaching!) into darkness always waiting. Single eyeball spinning above head like a perfect coin—treasure dragged from the animal, a nightmare jewel pushed back into face. Goddess dressed in purple death, a fly with 300 eyeballs.

In the mountains above the city, an adulteress murders her lovers among immortal magazines. The jealous lung ripped open like a rune dipped in red-black blood. Coils of white electricity appear in her eyes like fried sperm. The spinal column holding up Kuala Lumpur spacecraft—Disneyland pink periscope. We switch cutlery so not to be seen, knives pummelled through our bladders. Look into the camera and disappear into new and byzantine bruises.

Behold, it said, *Antarctica upon the skin, a horse inside its frostbitten stomach. Its mouth filled with red father meat.* Eating as paparazzi, kisses spilling with rats & cherries.

An actress undresses before an albino dressed in Georgian smock into a darkness always purple. To watch the dance of Salome and live longer. We look upon the mirror's face as a gigantic pink Lamborghini. Vanity moves further into red endlessness.

An unwashed dick end tasted by conjoined Aquarians. I cannot see their faces beyond the camera, just a cannibal speaking the liquorice sadness of the sun. It reveals pornography of jejunum and the green palace of spinal Nri. Incest led upon a table; dresses me in obedient ribbons. It drinks my ear—Hamlet slave hearing prophecy of shivered castle ghoul, a blank cackle upon the screen! Our house is now haunted!

.

.

.

WHEN AN ANGEL SEES ITS OWN REFLECTION, IT BECOMES A DEMON

.

Barbatos, Focalor, Amon. Autumn with its jaw flung open like a horse, the women fell to pieces in those laughing skies with throats devoid of sunlight or moon. Libras freezing in white vinyl gloves. The morning was frightened to ignite—children sewn into bin bags, refuse as formless as the whole house. Florida repented to blank water running through a garden, the silent daybreak. Through the trees it approaches in a tuxedo pressed by a woman with hands littered with sunspots and amethyst.

Kennedy Space Centre broadcast of a typewriter in an empty apartment writing its own death sentence. Orange face screaming on the ceiling. Franz Kafka resurrected during the Botticelli takeover. He tip-toed across a skyward bruise and leaped from her concrete family into pink Jupiter fog. Words still wet on the page. **A ghost came to dance through the narrow streets of Jaffa.**

It lives inside an infiltrated renaissance.

Her dreams are blue and pink wires—shattered blood, Mediterranean clouds. Sardinian hallway into grandmother hands holding wartime quartz. Tells a Nazi curse of men gilded in black dead flies. Holds an emerald to the light and speaks a name. **Paimon, Zepar, Zagan** dressed in white tunics. Evil is always the colour of Tokyo paradise. She holds her granddaughter close and tells her the password, sends her into the orchard.

Don't wear strong perfume at night, especially around trees. Don't wear your hair down, especially around trees. Don't sing. Don't recite anything that sounds beautiful for they will possess your body and they won't leave because they love you.

.

I see the sun expanding into a red skull covered in charcoal Picasso insects. Celebrities praying to a blue trapeze of blood. We daydream our way through bored classrooms like braindead cowboys—*youth is hunger*, said a fortune cookie, tossed from the car window into the desert: Brothels spilling with plasma transfusions from fainting tourists. A vampire sat in a leather harness, can taste the difference in sodium levels. Lipstick paused above the smoking revolver, limp cocks heavy as water lilies and wilted from Japanese denim. In silence we watch OLIVER TWIST SPRAYED IN RAT CHLORINE, abducted by a yellow-magenta UFO, his red bowels clutching around the endoscope enlarged upon the screen, its celebrated poverty. Roses starve too at night outside an abandoned cinema, empty beneath skies filled with dancing steam. Their village prince rising above London hell, decked in fresh garbage—twinkling Shinjuku radioactivity. iT sLEEPS pUZZLED aND aLONE aT nIGHT iNSIDE a mICROWAVE. Awaiting pylons, dreaming beef-pigs synthesised beneath red eclipse through feverish network of sugar-fuelled friction, Mars explodes above Yorkshire into ugly balloons. Blubberhouses. The sun-SKULLS (X): ten-headed machine never to look upon, its halo-warp downloaded from an internet cafe in Damascus, the Persian script coded and ran vertically along mountaintop graves. An ambitious slave whittled down to one screaming black skeleton, a billboard for a boy ozoned to death at a hairspray factory.

J. M. Barrie dreaming beneath a Scottish fir. He sees a Glasgow moon and sun, both brothers. *If you shut your eyes and are a lucky one, you may see at times a shapeless pool of lovely pale colours suspended in the darkness.*

Our furniture rises up tall now. Messages flickering on the screen like mayflies. We are dead and yet we speak for we are television, night dreams of the hallucinating X.

Murder the sun.

The dishwasher is a portal into Antarctica. Orange globes rise above forgotten & frozen plates as wide and silent as blood.

She remembers giving birth to doves drowned in cream. Holding each in her arms as though they were dead. To give birth to a horse and hear it running within. Red and turquoise feathers spewing from its open mouth—teleports into a massacred limousine in Shanghai, a leather attaché case lined with pink explosives. Hong Kong gasped into purple dawn.

Nikola Tesla in Colorado staring into a future dynamo coil—sat alone in his final sadness, undressed in a lead bucket. Tesla approaches a horse (my mother) dressed in a blue shingle and victory. To summon electricity directly from a plank of wood waiting to burst.

She is a ghost and sees herself on the Campus Martius in Ancient Rome, neck hacked and spewing juniper and raspberry before a roaring spaceship, the body beheaded in honour of Mars. An executioner covered in cobwebbed sweat speaks of an oak tree, of castrated Luppiter.

Flamines in red robes dance around the October horse, tossing silver dung into air. Her soma covered in black lice and butterflies.

She sees Nicholas II of Russia stolen from the gunpowder cellar, cowering with family and transported into the future. Metatron flowing in silver piss. Christian X of Denmark clone leaving seraphim chamber, his body swims through the spinning orb, arms dipped in Chinese platinum. Jupiter is a machine programmed to hijack and overthrow the sun (X), its ten terrible heads boiled alive inside Zhongma Fortress.

She sees THE FOURTH LIGHT IV still singing of the BAPTIZER as it awaits at the bottom of *the lake of melancholia, the lake of purple north, the dead lake of Pluto*. She laughs and throws her earrings in the way of gullible UFOs.

Let light take its time to reach us from God.

OCTOBER EMERGE

*

I am a Glasgow moon (*) and most sick. The moon returned to Los Angeles in a blue suitcase on fire. My head is made of heroin and rotates stricken and crippled in vat of orange plasma. To dance with four Bergman sisters and suffocate inside a pink phantasm, clouds of mourning doves bursting from an Ingrid windowsill, oilbirds all shot to pieces upon the stage.

A scorpion (myself), a horse (my mother), a bird (my father) switched places on Halloween inside a purple-green cobweb inside many rooms, acid-trinity: *the clown, the poet, the butcher.*

We arrive at the watchtower of the clown at the end of blue peyote poisons, flammable owls burst into Yaxchilan ash.

.

Bonampak prostitute teleports onto MTV-fluorescent bleach, anabolic aliens humming outside a seething Instagram glow. I spin inside hooker blue to become amphetamines inside Leningrad hole. Andy Warhol trapped in a dead oubliette, Holly & Candy (* *)—Glasgow sun and moon both kaleidoscopic like corkscrewing sleeves: hooker harlequin, malachite mantis. The green celebrities eat Yankee mad eyes of a tiger and toilet bowls filled with penicillin offered to a turtle god. Through magazine Adderall-sickness, we came to know wealth, became sewage oligarchs in a perpendicular Manhattan. Chrysler whores passed through duodenum, jejunum, ileum of a suited imp. Soft and pouting boy bruise, another head drilled apart like a godless pineapple. O endless lakes of food. We become pipes.

.

The distance between Jupiter and Io is 628,30000 km. We measure it with our fingertips as the salt-packed body of Christ is laid before us covered in father blood and ice. It tiptoes across the sticky carpet slickened with wasps. Condoms rolled backwards into dreaming sperm.

We dance before the shrine of **Saint Narcissus of Gerona** for our hands are wide and telekinetic—Carrie covered in sickle cells, a princess exploding into fire. She sells catalogues at the entrance.

Metatron abandoned in seawater spills through sockets of the house. We hear the headless songs of canned salmon. A bored angel. Dorothy levitating above a limousine massacre, eyes turned bad. It decays our teeth and we giggle! to watch the obese burst apart!

Surgical documentaries about billionaires tied and pumped with squid ink. News footage of a dodecahedron sun spinning on fumes imported from Hangzhou.

Lady Diana praying to become a Fuzanglong dragon as Catholic lilac smoke jumps across the chauffeur. He becomes a blue boil the size of a house. £86,000 car lurches through manufactured time into Hawaii, polystyrene Huixtocihuatl tossing salt at a blinding roadside— *cylinder, piston, & head* split into triptych, 3-headed Pele thrown from vehicle into emergency cot.

Plastic surgeons pull back Christ's face into aqua transsexual smiling inside the warm glow of a flashing and orange meteorite, now white in the centre of 3Y3BALL vortex. She survived and became a god of psychographic, ushering followers into a purple pyramid into their chosen sarcophagi. We are resurrected and unable to end, banshees choked on Manchester greed. Colours are acrylic saints again murdered, injected into its face—the Botox Mussolini on everyone's lips. Shredded against a lamppost, the television crew saw its soul was graffiti.

.

First

                                        we remove the slut apple,
                        pop it out
    like a zit

                        (head of a lollipop).
                                                Scribble
                lipstick
    across the exposed skull,

                                        doodle
boredom

                                        on the marrow
                        of its arms—
        ripped off
in seconds,

                        devour each hungrily
            in our
            open

                                neon

mouths.

                                        Fake eyelashes

                                                for the
daddy corpse

                                                        of
course.
                Chew them up
                    like bubble gum.
                                        His blood is pink.

It spoke of the purple north and she loved to hear it lie (lying! lying!) of worlds beyond the far side palace. Gnomes sunk inside black fire, a water devil peeling and asleep in a radiation den, its argon glowing nest. She had chosen the blonde head with twelve freckles paused upon the cheek at each hour, noontime constellation growing and spreading across the banquet hall like spider scent of tar and lavender causing the maids to fall asleep in their master's laps, groins that dream only of sequined duck feather. Plates of ruined bison stuffed with sage, rabbits peeled and pink, eyeballs left untouched by a queen covered in seeing jewels, a monstrous head twisted on like a vase. She span around the room, danced (dancing! dancing!) through the arms of feeble princes staring across plates of warm gruel, her hated lovers stood still beneath the mirror thief and the flower sewn into its white coat: a green rose, unseen in the Nri kingdom until now, the court muttering of other planets and moons as she wished herself (wishing! wishing!) into a new head, one more time. Red dawn spilling through the castle windows like jealousy—only to face her own reflection, horrid and screamed to see herself: the Eyeball Countess, a horrid stump. She ran from the room and ordered the thief seized, ashamed—a girl again, she wept from stolen eyes that alone she stabbed open with a bloodied pebble, felt them run (running! running!) red with all her borrowed treasure, saw the sun rise through her own murdered face. Every iris was auburn and must be destroyed.

JOHN THE BAPTIZER is the fourth of its kind, perfected in a Tokyo laboratory, emerges from a tank of electric eels, face blinded with battery acid. Pacific saury with open mouths spilling thorium—blue futures dragged forwards into 61-promethium, Christian Bale cauterised into Terminator blob.

A warehouse filled with titanium slaves worship the silver ball hovering in the exact centre of room, a silent camera authorised by San Francisco totem sat in a puddle of bronze filth. My mother (a unicorn) sees the Lithuanian cooling towers crack like blue-white eggshell, the TRANS-URANIUM RIVER FLOWING ACROSS A BALTIC CHILD, the morning sea boiled pink and white. The arms move in unison. Breathing, they hold each other at night beneath orange Soviet poverty, cherry trees fainting into tourism, cities filled with violet enema. Nightclubs with curtseying girl-coy hybrid, scaled body torn apart with bloodied hooks beneath clapping madman, sperm in her hair and pseudo-fins. Do you like my many toes and the water they tread upon? Her arms are shining as they are pulled from the sockets.

.

A scream as JOHN THE BAPTIZER teleports into 1918.

Nicholas II and his family are asked to get dressed and led into a basement. Yakov and Grigory reaching for a handgun. The air paused around a single bullet. Christian X of Denmark clone leaving chamber, switched with his doppelganger wearing the Royal Order of the Seraphim and smiles into a convex mirror. Anastasia, Tatiana, Olga and Maria found dead with jewels sewn into clothing (transmitted onto a haunted hill in 1609—asleep together inside new green skins). a mACHINE oBSESSED wITH lov3 tWISTS iTS oWN hEAD off like a lightbulb, its Tesla-unlocked exorcism. Our house is a cemetery of angels all facing east at dusk, light flown backwards. Glasgow moon drowned in the lake of melancholia.

.

.

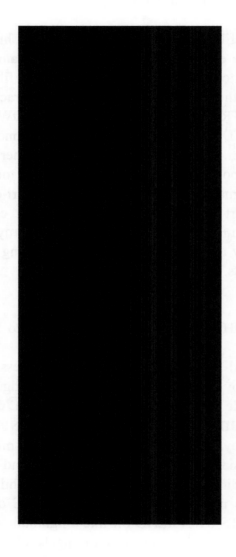

MIRROR III

A HORSE DESCENDS INTO LAKE OF MELANCHOLIA

We are conjoined now by only *slowness*. I reach my hand through the vast walkway along the thousand-wide bodies of horizontal furniture dipped into still and black lakes of Pluto—trafficked organs of a nitrogen witch. We live in a haunted house and the piano, banished into satanic silence at the bottom of the Tethys Ocean, hums its final oath. We hold candlesticks, dumbstruck & trembling to find our way from the kitchen to hallway, afraid to touch a garden statue of a Celtic sith, a horrible elf crawled from the rock. Its arm melted the arm into blood and through the water it whispered like blue trance as a Colorado laboratory burst into flames.

O come obese fire.

Swans float upon despised black scum as we pass tropics of inconstancy sunken beneath. Manhattan emerging, covered in red Brazilian flu, chickens sent into space like laughing debris. Shadows became ash across the surface of the table top—all convulsing like gibbons, chairs burst into calcium powder, their embarrassed insides. To live amongst and know one is being deceived by a cushion, its cycloptic gibberish, one-eyed & yellow. The clock is chiming XII as we stop to watch an old man unfold into smiling light, mouth huge and bursting through the collar, undresses in a lead bucket and waits for epiphanies. The hands and feet fall off first. We sink lower and lower into them: the blackness of a sun-SKULL (X) that swallows the bottom of the sea.

Sadness like a watermelon seed buried in a human heart.

Dripping in blood, chained to a Cenozoic temple block—an angel screams at the jealous cloud.

.

61

1. A PEACOCK-VAMPIRE BURIED ON PLUTO, 1917

2. GOD-X MACHINE (X FURIOUS HEADS OF SUN)

3. ELECTRICITY BECOMING THE BLOOD OF SWORDFISH

.

The dying world accepted tulips & Mississippi lawns spray-painted green, beauticians worsened into surgeons. tHEY iNJECT pROGRAMMED bLUE jARGON iNTO lIMBIC bLADDER— twitching as expanded into drooling gloss, blood tiaras crushed into snow. Fathers fucked and painted in acrylic wash.

I outlive Alaska and rise into Beijing skies to dance madly among pollution and purple goblins, howl with *penanggalan* and *manananggal* far beyond Indonesia.

We feed on pig corpses and fly—stretch miles-long into chewing gum. We are weightless vampire bodies summoned beneath a pink Indian moon, levitating above wooden huts of a tropical plateau. Nightmares breathing in one blue cave. At school we masturbated into the arms of vending machines: Fanta Limon, Fanta Grape, Lucozade-melted heaven.

I wank at orange clouds sliding across the screen. My prick facing the Miami loop on fire. To masturbate with a murdered, trembling laser moving across Blambangan king corpse covered in blue bumblebees. The mummified Saint Catherine of Bologna surrounded by gold Triassic angels peering over her rotten black feet.

Leprechauns gamble the soul of a beluga, its damnation sealed beneath the Arctic Ocean.

I peer into the sheet of glass and see Lucifer like
a hummingbird on fire.

Ornias transforms from a vampire into a peacock. Metatron eats the
whole of Japan, becomes a concrete Kether.

.

TENTH SUN-SKULL (X)

EYEBALLS (CCC) IN BUBBLE GUM SKULL

NRI GREEN PALACE OF (COMPUTER) INCEST

She has chosen her prettiest head (XII) from the glass cabinet and saw (seeing! seeing!) envy in the eyes of the others—to be adored by a creature and watch her legs spread open to slithering moonlight, stars circling above like hungered red mayflies. She had bathed her body in almond and honey, saw again how she had always been correct and drank the crystalline hex, wore a poisoned brooch clipped into her false white hair. She hammered the skull of an ice empress onto her spine, eyes as sapphire as dawn and filled (filling! filling!) with tears to see her love move through the wall of the castle courtyard, silver evening light tangled and cobwebbed inside its cold mouth. Running towards the mirror thief, she could already feel the gown slip (slipping! slipping!) and she was naked sex now and no longer dead, filling herself with its tongue and hands, lips pulled back and cold. Its tongue moved through her like a shard of glass and she saw (seeing! seeing!) again the silence of the sun, all one hundred eyeballs of hers turned upward at skies above the far side palace. A fuck witch unblinking, faced the emptiness of pink heaven, a wound spilling blood and light. She wept at dinner as it placed the silver ring in her hand and fell (falling! falling!) to its knees. A hundred eyes sobbing together, her miserable hair flowing with joy.

Ten red centipedes crawled across the sun (X), amoebas trapped and headless on the screen—twisting. Henna-ridden slaves of King Herod sat atop the laughing castle of Jabneh.

My mother (a horse) sensed the fluorocarbons rushing down her spinal T-1 into T-2, the technicolour neck plug of JOHN THE BAPTIZER spewing out green Daiichi warnings. Ambient hiss of cattle scrambled into shapes. It sees their bodies washed and led out like glowing rabbits, cathode slurry running through a body until it teleported into chromium batteries—into Sala Ni Yalo (Germanic red-pink caves). A microwave open and filled with yellow sperm. We undress inside steam, snow monkeys boiled into mince.

An angel torn apart in a vat of beef, flogged by the butcher (my father) and his seeing hounds.

My mother (a poet) falls through a shadow into 1889. 3Y3BALL rolled back in the skull, winter crashing onto coldest stars above that begin to move! and condense into a scream! We warp into obesity—witness a Neptune alien on fire in the hallway.

My mother reaches across and kisses a scarlet macaw stapled to the wall, its breast covered in electric blue topaz, face peeled away into rainbow lorikeet.

.

.

From the water it emerges, born in silver hatred and orange lava, risen in Valles Marineris, Capri Chasm. She flings open the dishwasher and finds the northern bald ibis sat alone in darkness. Its hooked, pink head, hideous atop black plumage: the first bird released from the ark of Noah, a seer of death.

Its wings are open.

It floats above a black sea, a billion beneath the cannibal glass—the confessing dead.

My mother falls in love with the D3ATH MACHINE.

Luppiter swollen at each stroke, its noontime body rubbed in charcoal. Mercury funnelled through organs kept in glass tanks, the Tamagotchi face programmed to beg.

She measures the distance between herself and Io frozen and smashed into heroin. A lesbian mouth sealed in mascara. My mother (a horse) swims and sinks into chat shows, coughed and bleary.

Blue bubonic plague, armpits filled with purple rats.

Her body is an arrow. She reveals the insignia of her own mistrust. A human heart given to the machine: a fist of meat dipped like a rune in red-black blood.

In Hindu Kush mountains, an adulteress murders the other villagers for their persecution, crashing a flint down onto a vibrating pile of skulls. Haggard vultures dressed in sapphires make love and dissolve inside the hissing nimbus, a hive of air spells. The flesh is stripped clean in minutes by fire ants. AN ENTIRE SKULL POPS OPENS LIKE A RAT TRAP AS LOCUSTS ROAR INTO A FEVERISH SKY FLECKED WITH LIVING SPIRALS OF BLOOD. Father (a vampire) falling asleep as the house fades into NCG 1409.

We watch the jungle-red torture, a girl tied to ten-foot bamboo pole aside of a riverbed. Soul aborted in a white flash of lightning. She waits. Her body is an arrow. The crocodiles will be swimming downstream at the first sign of light. A preacher screaming from Honduras swamp, insect prism of night dreams. A yellow ribbon floats in his open palm.

.

Aurea handed a pigeon in Spanish, shit-filled cave. She crawls through hexamita, chlamydia, her paradisal daughters.

.

Woman enters kitchen.

Woman: Boy, am I tired of washing these.

Holds up white shirt covered in the blood of the villagers.

Woman: I wish there was some way of removing these damn stains.

Dishwasher opens, begins to speak.

Dishwasher: Mother, we are dead and yet we speak.

Bubbles of purple and pink begin to froth from the machine.

To live and die inside hypnosis. Light spinning around each computer like pristine haloes, cadavers embalmed in yellow and blue.

The pregnant body of Mary hijacked into garbled, green gossip.

.

.

A bigot ascends a podium in ill-fitting blood transfusions: a tenth of a Mexican smuggled across the border, poisonous and cold. Welcomed with a bouquet by face-lifted abracadabra, he speaks in five . . . four . . . three . . . *I don't want some union delegate telling me when to get on and off the elephant.* And there lay the faces of many, upturned to blinding heaven like escalators. Holding out a sunflower towards them, he weeps with euphoria. *What if plants and the trees became fascists too?*

.

A blood clot on fire. We turn from white ozone blasted into a Tokyo child staring into spheres spinning at the crimson end. An angel dreams only in television images, blue antenna glued to spine. Sat in Shinjuku hovel, the Holy Spirit rising from an empty beer bottle—wings tipped with motorcycle rubies.

A demon covered in methane returned from the Taiwanese dead: cybernetic-Lazarus drunk on lithium stumbles from the hospital ward into daylight. A bad moon crashing into a grave of wands.

The child is bald and happy—asleep inside a pterodactyl.

.

On their wedding night, each of her heads howled with envy from the cold glass cabinets to watch (watching! watching!) the Eyeball Countess lead her silver husband into the castle keep, bed littered with jasmine flowers, lemongrass—her neck plug oiled with grapefruit and cinnamon. It saw the metal throat threaded with yellow ribbons, her body sagging beneath the nervous magic woven from a zebra barely alive in a bedroom cage, its solemn eyeballs: one blue, one green—a familiar stolen from the Mongolian wizard, eaten (eating! eating!) his sockets from the ancient skull, zebra neighed (neighing! neighing!) to see a beloved master broken into salt. She turned (turning! turning!) to reveal herself, a fantasy rotten and fed on the young blue visions of others, only to see the reflection of herself (seeing! seeing!) led upon the bed, naked and transformed. The mirror thief was now her own terrible form, a torso covered in swivelled (swivelling! swivelling!) eyeballs all turned backwards, shaking as it laughed (laughing! laughing!) at the countess frozen in horror, her gallery of heads screaming in unison as felt the dagger plunge into her heart—the murdered, eyeless skulls all sealed shut.

In the stark light of Miami cypress, pond apple—yellow blooms in her hair, palm leaves folded into Sunday demon.

Pollen like a hurricane gasping awake. Molten steel simulacra of parasitic Virgin Mary cradling sacred red worms.

My mother descends in gloves of slaughtered fox into che-quered water like an evil pirouette balanced on the balls on its heels.

Princess Peach with mouth smeared in anti-green, trans-dimensional potions. When the soul of a child is stolen, the tribe turns to the angakkuq. Suns gulped into an empty windowpane like breathing spores, castle covered in red rooms bursting into bird flu.

On webcam, we sleep in silent dormitories, tied in & dreaming Argento screams! We are October children born beneath a solar wind blowing from the north, elsewhere and polka.

.

A drumbeat through the village waking us from our beds for there is no way back into summertime, autumn with its mouth flung open like a horse. We know what the music means and men in jackets their grandfathers once hated. Each holding a flag to October unkind. Just the steady march and the horses braying softly (thy helium eyes).

Every child born in the month of October was rounded up and hanged from the neck.

Our little shoes, all dropping off.

.

.

MIRROR IV

A HORSE DESCENDS INTO LAKE OF PURPLE NORTH

I am a chequered harlequin born in green smoke and I come from the north. Banshees eaten on Nome orphans look upon sunflowers burst open into blood, (X) factory heads becoming tuberculous.

An angakkuq studies every person present because an evil spirit can take on the form of a good spirit.

A doppelganger enters the Inuit feast. Arctic char littered with salt and cloudberry, a muskox leg boiled in face gravy. We look upward at blank and broken satellites that record the rate of extinction, GRAPHS PLUNGING SKYWARD LIKE RED TERROR BIRDS.

Canadian technocrat licking green boreal cocaine, confirms his mission to build a transparent hell. The angakkuq reads the tattooed chest of a Brooklyn curse, a Puerto Rican lizard cuckoo. Tyrant tied to a desk chair—mouth fucked apart by cryptocurrencies like screaming purple hyena.

She splits in two like silent twins and drinks his brains (!), veins torn out and fed into wasp shit. (* *)

Mouth beamed directly across into Helsinki radio station. Images on screen of Vancouver bastille dragged into purple north, Christian Bale flexing at a wall socket. A television surgeon sliced apart at a black equator.

My father walks into Sala Ni Yalo (a yellow room).

Kafka sank into the Nigerian hotel floor.

We sit among blazing crows fallen into sleep and night. The angakkuq removes a box carved from beluga tusk, a glass cube empty except for a floating jewel: the death token. An emerald to summon pandemonium. Face peeling away into red bleeding corvette, sulphuric poisoned heaven.

O come obese fire. She sees the glass head. *The human soul is female,* she whispers, dissolves into blue fog. We forget Europe, there are only moons.

Metatron>>led in an orange coffin>> fed into greedy clouds.

.

At the stroke of XII we bathe in deaf Brazil—THE FOURTH LIGHT IV. Autumn with its mouth flung open like a horse banished from land and drowned in the Tethys Ocean.

God (a monster) had tied four Cenozoic temple blocks to the hooves of a horse, its mane covered in blue shingle and victory. An angel writing in a golden book about the miraculous aspects of things existing: naked bodies of Grigori covered in sunspots and amethyst falling through tectonic Valais plates, Uriel warning Noah through orange magma portal of Ornias dipped in black latex like homosexual prince, the carved off head of Thoth.

A woman (angakkuq) speaks through blue fog: don't wear strong perfume at night, especially around trees. Don't wear your hair down, especially around trees. Don't sing, don't recite anything that sounds beautiful. They will possess your body and they won't leave because they love you.

I wash on a silent footpath next to a Derbyshire river, waiting alone with hair caked in soil and insects.

Here comes a demon.

Barbatos, Focalor, Amon.

I lie back and unfurl as perfect as water.

Paimon, Zepar, Zagan.

My skin is silver.

SOUL | FIRE

MIRROR
(HORUS 3Y3BALL)

The hexagon bastard had become bored with his powdered servants, had all bowed (bowing! bowing!) before their headless countess had hit the ground, her seeing pearls scattered across the castle keep, twelve heads shrivelled (shrivelling! shrivelling!) into black skulls, a diamond sealed in each mouth: gift from the east, jealous tama stolen from the lair of a green dragon. It used a kind blade to bleed (bleeding! bleeding!) the sycophantic court. They howled to watch a pierrot dance upon burning coals, his mouth sealed in pig wax. It approached the mirror, long and thin with arms like shining knives and saw (seeing! seeing!) blue futures. Spilling from the glass, another soul reached out to escape glittered hell—the family of Nicholas II of Russia shivering in a basement, Yakov and Grigory grasping for the handgun. Anastasia, Tatiana, Olga and Maria, four sisters screamed (screaming! screaming!) around a single bullet moving through space and time as glass burst (bursting! bursting!) in the face of the mirror thief. It was four sisters transmitted onto a haunted hill in 1609, it was Christian X of Denmark clone leaving chamber, switched with his doppelganger wearing the Royal Order of the Seraphim and smiled (smiling! smiling!) into the silver mirror. A Uranian King, a fly with 300 eyeballs.

My mother (a poet) had eaten the eyeballs from the locust-stuffed head of JOHN THE BAPTIZER. Insects aluminium and programmed in its Hangzhou laboratory, set aflight amongst bright trenches of methamphetamine, slaughterhouse offal hung like jewellery upon the cow stuffed with blue cocaine.

She saw it rise up amongst pink carrion, mouth stuffed with perfect oaths, wings tipped with motorcycle rubies—stares across Osaka harbour. Holy Ghost rising from champagne flute, a Scottish baptism crashed onto the forehead of startled babe, an aqua-Christ turned cyan and evil inside Edinburgh sewer. My brothers are the Glasgow sun and the Glasgow moon, switched each side of the computer screen.

I see Proust and Flaubert twist into flubber like blue hurricanes masturbating into and with hollow light.

It was the first day of a Yonville summer and Madame Bovary awakens in outer space.

Dazed, she masturbates into long comets, the sordid and everlasting afternoon. She sees A MONSTER STUMBLE THROUGH A FIELD AMONGST FLEUR-DE-LIS, mouth black and agape, cock covered in dragonfly shit. *Another daydream*, Charles Bovary repeats, smiling into the Kuiper Belt. Nitrogen tetroxide eating through their insides, the shattering of teeth. Her skull exploded at noon—she saw death as a hot pink Lamborghini. UFOs balanced atop the glittering carcass of Berthe Bovary, a daughter born into the month of October, blonde omen speaking from the wooden chair. *Never give a knife as a gift, never cross a stream holding a cat.*

Her dreams are blue and pink. She was in love.

Her body is an arrow (>>) and she sees the hexagon coming out of her, spinning and green with ten heads: dodecahedron.

She follows her feet and toes into the mirror of her own creation, a monster that screamed the scream she had inside her throat when spanked, screamed from its own little mouth—its tiny chandelier teeth.

Tattoo of a cherry blossom on an opioid addict, soft glass filled with Accrington smog. Welcomed into Lancaster fortress by the turquoise arms of a yaksha.

It rises from the hostel floor, sipping a bottle of Fanta. Face still warm from dashing across red valleys. They make love to dappled canalside spouses. Bodies combined beneath colossal supermarket, bhoots dissolved in the plaza outside Argos. Their sleeves hiccup nitrogen (N2) and carbon dioxide (CO2) as spindly twigs of factory chimneys snap under gravity poured into molten air. An ozone god suffocating in a Preston prison teleports into Nyenchen Tanglha mountains, dressed in shattered Christmas blood.

A girl in Arkansas called Ama stolen from Ghana, watches a cotton boll turn pink in her bloodied palm.

The land is under the spell of a snake charmer. Endless canals and sound of pungi-like reeds call the yaksha to the motorway bridge with his backwards feet. It steals miracles. Lancaster witches stood beneath Asda glowing like Mongolian jade, speak the demdike mutter. *The edges of a black hole are called soft hair.* She reaches through time and holds her own daughter, old now—a hag covered in red lice, arms like melted fat; flickering grandmother screwed on the BAPTIZER head awoken inside the voodooed microwave. Darkness descends on Burnley as Lucifer rides out across motorway bridges, teleports into Accrington—a megaparsec gULPED iNSIDE tHE pETROL sTATION aTTENDANT. The stars are moving away from us.

.

MIRROR V

A HORSE DESCENDS INTO DEAD LAKE OF PLUTO

JOHN THE BAPTIZER screws on his final head (XII) and looks into the sun, sees only black honey—his own beautiful cunt.

Ornias dipped in black latex levitating above mountain like homosexual flowers bursting through windowsills littered with droppings. A telescope points at Pluto which my father (a bird) crawls towards, my mother sinking beneath into Japanese microbes. Castle rooms painted in purple glyphs: **an ibis bended inside a crushed square**, faces pressed against sapphire coffins, tubes into head and arms. Each liberated into coldness, the sadism of the machinating moon.

She wanders through corridors peering at the geishas fed on butterfly protein, pulls back the canvas screen to meet her own sister.

Post-Antigone with stainless vertebrae swivelling around like rat snake, eyes leaking hornet venom, mumbles a perfect oath: マシンムーン .

The moon is made of heroin and birthed in Kuchinoerabu, silver orb hovering above the hand of Ophelia slave emerging from a bathtub of eel slime, 3Y3BALL5 blue and endlessness.

We only wish for your love, a promise of sleep: come and lie in the centre of the moon, inside Antarctica. Judas (a scorpion) born into ice and eaten in the mouths of Lucifer with Cassius (a horse) and Brutus (a bird), winter eternal. Look into the skies and see Pluto risen above a Beijing skyscraper, four sisters undressed in programmed Gethsemane, a mOTHER sWAN pULLED aPART iTS oWN hEART tO fEED iTS yOUNG oN rED-pINK bLOOD. She lives again as a monitor, blissful simulation.

Selfish and red. A rectum as eternal as money.

The mirror thief was crowned on the first day of summer, sunlight shined (shining! shining!) on the blood tiara which dripped upon its satin slippers, laughter run red from the keep into a song-filled throne room, silver webs of good fortune spun by a white imp: seer into air, beyond the far side palace into purple night. Thread of hair fed into the mouth of the imp, cried (crying! crying!) to see fire waiting beneath the palace, its haunted rooms filled with graves. A water dragon asleep beneath the keep, wriggling in obnoxious treasure, the slippers of a telekinetic witch. There was only sleep, a coronation of opium-burst poppies. A machine wheeled out, a golden box that conjured a green princess, an angel at the end of the mountain. The mirror thief stared into the sun (staring! staring!) and saw only its own face broken into pieces, strangled the white seer until he burst into bats. It looked into the glass—liquid night and entered (entering! entering!) the deranged mirror, a prince eaten into walls, tiptoed towards the edge of the castle balcony and leaped into pink Jupiter fog, the infiltrated renaissance.

A HORSE DESCENDS INTO A BLUE HELL IN ZHENGZHOU COMPUTER

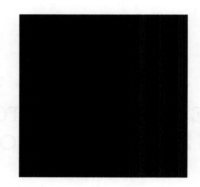

III

SCARECROW KING

(a bird—corpse covered in golden lice)

"O! you silent mirrors of truth.
On the elfin-boned temple of the lonely one
Appears the reflection of fallen angels."

— Georg Trakl, Night Song

EARTH

My father (a bird) was born at the final stroke of noon into complete darkness—in a red cellar with iron shutters closed tight for she (flickering! flickering!) knew noon to be green hypnosis—the faces of the sun-SKULL to be symmetry, the hatred of G0D-X (ten-headed, berserk), its mouths stuffed with springtime blood, an April clown on fire.

As she puffed and panted in labour, felt the child spilling out inside a pool of glass, a window conceived in the Lancaster cobbled street amongst furious & emeraldine rats and the dull light of a petrol station like a manatee sank alone into the ocean, motorways running through her amphetamine dream.

She had watched sperm boiled alive in a Blackpool jacuzzi.

They saw blind homosexuals grope into darkness always waiting, grottos beneath the sunken casinos. Their loving and miraculous piers burst into fire!

And she took off her red slippers to run into coldness, the radioactive Irish Sea. All the time dancing, dreaming of the Isle of Wight—merciful land of Jehovah. A Mormon bible filled with instructions to summon an evening-tide archangel. She mouthed an American curse as she pushed the baby through the Blackburn A666 pipeline, saw her own hallucinating clitoris.

.

A monster (a son) crawled beneath her feet. Yellow river that ran through the town over the faces of Jehovah's Witnesses erased against walls brightest in the month of October. A grandmother that dabbed her forehead and held a candelabra close to her as she delivered the screaming infant, flickering hag below the house. She saw through time into November treacle, years passing like rain. The creature whispered into her ear of the impregnation of a parasitic machine—Damascus ego-computer.

First words spoken from the grandmother to the babe.

The edges of a black hole are called *soft hair.*

.

Our round heads were filled at school with afternoon sums.

Each gobbling, algebra face. A pie chart divided into equal faces. An isosceles menace on the Samsung screen!

Spheres that peered into green Lagos internet cafe. A Nigerian demon downloaded—its skeleton body covered in sleeping sickness.

A rollercoaster tied to the broken back of St Martin. His mouth opening like chalice of blood. Poverty begged outside Pendle cul-de-sac, warheads shot into a Libyan camp, 3Y3BALLS blinded by HIV mist.

Lagos alchemist gathers immortal plastic inside a voodooed
microwave, sings the demdike mutter.

We run south towards a postcard built in the air by our hands, blood frozen inside claps of red thunder. A halo of flies twisting around each fourth son—the tuxedo hierophant at the front of the classroom explaining envy of photosynthesis, diagrams of seething jungle. Flowers are patient as we watch them wilt into shivering red pollen, slow breath of forest djinn. Made a wish upon a green rose for the computer to steal a human soul, face trapped on the screen in grainy grey and blue. A mauve boy undressed and wanked for King Herod and applauding statues, speakers strapped to the face and torso. Ornias speaks of his multiplying genitals, his pluralised beak. African sacred ibis (a poet) sings with the language of Jabneh, the 698 names of my mother (a water dragon).

.

We listen to the beheading of the October horse. The breath of a demon learning to speak—murder dreaming on a windowpane.

.

Its scales blazing like Dublin fire. I sink to the depths of the Irish Sea, embraced in lithium.

.

Florida repented to blank water running through the garden, orange pastor screaming on television of Pluto night! complicit satellite debris! Tourists deafened and smothered in Brazilian isotopes—white future light. A beach imported from a communist warehouse.

Kafka hiding in Palestine beneath a bad moon, falls asleep in lime green paradise.

To fuck the husband skull—look into its sapphire maxilla telling lies. The kissing dragon that granted immortality inside its Tethys currents.

His voice chanting . . .
my name . . . the name he chose for me . . .
chanting over and over again.

She opens the pristine browser into a corridor of Algerian boys—rivulets of frost melted in the mouths of pensioners amongst incestuous houseplants. She irons every last pillowcase and uploads images of a condom rolled down Japanese steel, her forearms syrupy with lubricant used by shy, pale equestrians. A witch brooch cleansed in water as she moves before the webcam, a face on the computer—a
blonde limousine, hag hair filled with money

spiders and blood transfusions shattered across the enormous windscreen, Irene (doppelganger) rushed across the Atlantic into Liverpool hotel. Her breasts bound with black latex. SHE SMILES INTO HER MUSEUM OF SHIVERING BOYS.

Betty screams! and wakes into a purple pollution cult. Werewolf smoke. A palindrome hurled into Antarctica.

*

Jeanne Bates, Naomi Watts. Daughters of Herod drinking Holy Ghost from a champagne flute. Turquoise Mombi, Queen X. Laughter.

BETTY: I sleep in a train carriage amongst crosswords that go backwards and forwards.

IRENE: *(All the passengers smile as they hurl into Antarctica.)* We live inside machines ambitious & allowed to think without human interference.

(Arms prickly with twilight spread across the ice. Betty points at the face outside the train window, a face howling into freezing wind.)

BETTY: An impostor!

THE FACE: *(mouthing)* An angel dreams inside a television.

(Betty reaches into her diplomat case for a weapon surrendered in white Himalayan flowers.)

IRENE: Acting is reacting so when they say it, I just react.

(Betty shoots bazooka through the glass at the enormous polar sun frothing in the sky like an orange-pink brain. A jellyfish gone mad.)

.

The mirror thief had fallen from the far side palace (falling! falling!) through the upside-down glass into beyond, a graveyard of skull and purple smoke, land of the Scarecrow King. Skeletons held green lanterns, bats moving across fullest Lucifer moon shining upon their shining bones, a lonely song (singing! singing!) through the air of sadness, the tale of kissing (kissing! kissing!) a spider upon the cemetery river, its web wrapped around a cold hand rose into the air. A lizard's heart frozen underwater into a fire opal. The mirror thief watched Hamlet gravediggers combust into black marrow, forever bones sighed (sighing! sighing) into dust, a crypt sank into the black earth, green night spilling across the statues frozen until morning, never to end. A kiss from the Scarecrow King and their eyes unblinking, became pale, dying (dying! dying!) forever as a stone figure, lost inside their blue crumbling dream, a cackling cancer. It reached for the face of the statue. a cherub risen out of forsaken ground. A single tear of glass frozen on its cheek—mouth torn off by dogs. The ground opened (opening! opening!) into invitation, an entrance into a silver labyrinth—a magician welcomed into the sorrow of rats.

A green wind moved through the house, all furniture swivelled towards the syphilitic prophet.

Paris Hilton plunged into platinum, head covered in mining bees.

Mozambican Lilith led across the backs of alligators, wallets carved from sanga, a skeleton tattooed on the throat of a mouse. She sings into Madagascar, red temple dust. **Kek and Kauket switching places inside a bathroom faucet,** a 4chan fascist sucked into frog hell. Their necks ulcered and burst with leopard orchid—Florida teen screaming into a webcam as yellow gazania explodes out of medulla, another misguided marijuana epiphany. **Qamishli gulped into air.**

.

A dishwasher that cleanses children sewn into bin bags—all sank into orange poverty, refuse as formless as the whole house. All knowing in the same voice: *October is the most cherished stomach.* A videotaped corpse that sank into their blessings. Metatron dressed in blue shingle descends from Aquarius constellation like turquoise Eurydice, summons Ornias from the scream of a vampire bat. I watch a knife sink into its flesh, the small chest of a father (a bird) that takes turns flying across the room, armchairs covered in other creatures drank in silver hair.

A seance of silent mothers, women that fell to pieces in those laughing skies. The orange coffin fed into silver fire, his final tangerine scream. They smoke heroin from a glass eyeball in Tripoli car park, WATCH NEBUCHADNEZZAR ABDUCTED INTO SPACECRAFT and rubbed in cleaning alcohol, arms flung open like arrows towards NGC 3242.

A jealous chandelier, the ghost of Jupiter.

.

.

.

I see my father (a bird-butcher) on the computer screen. Locked and frozen inside the tenth head of the sun-SKULLS.

An octopus-god guided by green Benghazi lasers into the open mouth of an Italian princess, flu virus mutating on a glass screen.

·

Napoli laboratory filling with purple light, nURSES dANCING aND cOVERED iN vANILLA, each a laughing smudge behind the curtain. My father (an ibis) had stared into a telescope and seen termites living in the walls, the lime in the brick that ate the house—THE FOURTH LIGHT IV (spheres at the crimson end) beamed down from Io swamp. He tiptoed across a skyward bruise and leaped from a concrete balcony into washed Jupiter fog, the moon in the window above his bed, its awful head swivelled round.

Peasants collecting snow in Stockholm where the spaceship landed. Kafka led into a hotel room where a typewriter writes its own death sentence. Words still wet and powerless upon the page. A ghost came to dance through the narrow streets of Jaffa. A door flings open and we stare into that yellow room. August Strindberg asleep in black light, sees a pond marbled with starved hair. The nameless in deaf gloves enter the yellow room. A revolver pressed into his neck, his arms pumped with argon. A horse demon with eyes of helium. They ask him questions about the red city, about his immunity. He finds his balding wife (Ingrid of Sweden) in dreams amongst dandelions, his children dead in a zoo.

The world has ended.

·

FREEZE OUR SOULS SO WE MIGHT SINK INTO BUMBLEBEES

·

When an angel sees its own reflection, it becomes a demon.

Its body (a bird) is hung from a hook and shredded into light, pink songs exploded at noon.

Tesla sat alone in silence watching the shivering glass. Wings tied to an electrical boll, smell of protein. Uriel (Wednesday) peeled open into fish, its Friday mouth blubbering of Tethys water.

Edinburgh streams as clear as dawn.

Glasgow spires corkscrewing into blue-pink morning.

My father (a master) sits in plastic above the computer screen. Sorcerer fed on cooked lizards, dinosaurs fried in apple lard. To see the Yucatan peninsula, an extinction of rats covered in black plague— Artaud asleep inside syphilis coma, machines hung with purple bags of lavender, reciting Parisian hex. Graveyards stacked with honeyed recruits, a homosexual dipped in black latex descends on Nigerian cloud. Skype portal into rainforest asphyxiation, tendril-laced boys naked and coughing the consecutive juju moons of Saturn. He sees his own children in a Sao Paulo zoo, scotopic tiger eyes that see through six walls. Hooker's harlequin, malachite mantis. A vampire waiting in lime green paradise.

Goblets full of octil and offered to a turtle god. Amnesia.

A slave fucked in dungeons below the Nyenchen Tanglha mountains. Each room beneath our house: the dungeon of umbrella pande-monium, *the dungeon of liquorice night, the dungeon of a yellow phantom.* I see my father (a bird) eat an emerald. Running south into T1-T2 spine hijacked into BAPTIZER machine speaking silver blood, neck stump baptised in bees.

Sat in obese jewellery, we forget our own names.

It had stepped into itself and saw (seeing! seeing) the limits of its own glass body, the pink haze around its longer marbled arms, eyelashes frozen as knife shards, the platinum blood circling in loops back and forth around its pale silent heart. It felt the backwards skull expand as it sank (sinking! sinking!) into the hallowed ground of a ruined graveyard into a pit covered in white crocus flowering through snow and dead dirt, the lips of children humming forgotten songs before the Scarecrow King, when the sun had closed its jaws. It ran into the silver labyrinth into swimming reflections, light again expanding (expanding! expanding!) around a single breath inside a dark corridor. A hallway flipped into a reversing castle, blue-green eyeballs switching in the head of a mute gnome that beckoned one forward. The mirror thief saw a doorway open. It crushed the gnome skull in its hand, felt the thankful yawn as indigo brain bloodied. It levitated across the disfigured corpse into pink chasm, an altar raised and covered in shatter, glass breaking (breaking! breaking!) into pieces. The scream of an innocent, a slave with bones of glass smashed open—a crystal swan born into blood.

Flies shift above our heads to form constellations. Zeus in electric-blue eels melted into an eagle preyed down on milk-white Ganymede flesh.

.

An agoraphobic twink uploaded to cartoon bliss fuck site, **gob-stopper hole raided with tongues,** the green head convulsing like red Venus flytrap.

My father swims into Aquarius, southernmost skies. Our house watched over by a turquoise and malevolent bird: morning as we reach the ziggurat temple. Charax memories fed on a skirting board. **The god Ea dissolves** inside an airing cupboard, cuboid Pegasus. Acrylic saints burst open into fluorescent lavatory flush, green-blue television. Hyper celebrities trapped in an ivied cage, their mouths moving in wallpapered fright, sing of pink Johannesburg.

My mother (a horse) breathing in the annex, becoming stronger as Sunday pours through the attic, glimpses Sala Ni Yalo (blood red lagoon). My father (berserk eagle) watching a blob of ectoplasm divide into clockwise midday angels and waltz at their cresting feet.

His blood-stained mothers all floated into bleach.

Quietly, died in a room alone—*astonished.*

From their ashes, rises dioxide air; the evil birth of spring.

.

BRAIN>>EYE>>HEART>>PHALLUS

I>>II>>III>>IV

FED INTO THE MACHINE

.

Manhattan stranger tears out parts from the daddy-boy, places meat on golden weighing scales. Indonesian spider-numbers scrolling on screen.

Fortune-conjoined Aquarians kissed as a Vegas skeleton swills haemoglobin from the laminated veins of his painted gigolo.

An IBM machine with a Garbo accent, a Caspar David Friedrich painting serving macrobiotic rice. A Warhol ghoul puts makeup on in the mirror, zombie rising in Roman tunic rising through a wormhole.

.

A few thousand py6 for Cara Delevingne protozoa, fresh from vectors off the coasts of Bosaso and Djibouti. We run into grapefruit sun-SKULL rising in the south. My father (a bird) fills the singing house with all his murdered daughters—sons and mothers that lined the walls with cocktail blood, DEATH SQUADS DRESSED IN VELLUM FOR A RAPID ANNIVERSARY. We see through the glass into orange corpse wading into heat. Mosquitos still crawling across the open mouth, white giraffes shot into potassium.

Japanese purple iris.

.

Lancashire valley filled with flame lilies swaying under the spell of a snake. A girl from Ghana watches bloodied hand dye a cotton boll pink.

.

Sun towering above like a gigantic pool of mercury. I smell its ash in my mouth. I taste cremating—the speaking urn! I open my mouth into red vertical children, Marrakech turned south away from the Atlas Mountains to show the second face of Janus, ignores his schizoid dream.

.

When my father (a vulture sat in sapphire) turned around at noon (hallway aligned with ten sun-SKULLS on fire) we saw the silent patience of furniture.

Armchairs waiting at extinct dawn.

An ashtray melting into obese light, the toxic blood of swordfish. Noon can never end—vertical children tied to a post during October night and shot in the face. Their vampire bodies summoned & harpooned beneath pink tropical moon, levitating above wooden huts on Mesoamerican plateau. We are the knights of young sperm, nightmares breathing in one blue cave. Scorpios forever.

A piano appears in the centre of the house. An angel climbs inside its fat Guatemalan body, amongst spiders rushing through its emptied brain filled only with July wires and songs of a selfish forest. The angel wants to scream, watching the hammer strike another string tightening around its flesh! ivory keys torn from the heads of elephants! A cherub pressed flat into urgent lines, strangled inside the red web.

We torture an angel over and over. O death, where is thy sting? O grave, where is thy victory? *The sting of death is sin.* A northern bald ibis was the first to see the water flow. We eat chickens berserk and feathered, crushed inside the voodooed microwave. To tear off flesh from a human body and hear songs beneath—behind the xylophonic cadaver floated in air, a bird-of-paradise flying into space. It knows the Lamborghini-soul to always be female and on fire.

Look into a mirror and see a flock of murdered cockatoos, yellow sun conures smashed into window panes, A RAINBOW LORIKEET DRENCHED IN HOT AND SPOKEN BRAINS.

My mother sings of *Luppiter:* the true name of god, the bird that carried Zeus's envy. a bLUE nECKLACE cOMING tHROUGH tHE wALLS. Electrons. We die again and again in jewellery, the sorry poetry of flies. Midnight appears and we remain: green and dreadful cousins of noon. Tokyo witches melted at the platinum factory.

MIRROR VI

A BIRD SINGS IN THE DUNGEON OF LIQUORICE NIGHT

We live in a haunted house with the master in his glass tower and the LOV3 MACHINE asleep in its diamond cage, murder dreaming on the looking glass. We eat through leather straps pulled across our torsos, ribcages vandalised with crayon: blue, green, red prophecies of San Francisco health and sunlight. There is only a slow rotation of midnight now—indigo gondolas sank into liquid shit beyond Venice moonlight.

Our hands clawing through the corridors of the sanatorium littered with broken walls and windows. A concrete bollard carved in the car park into necro-father, dead scarecrow-god hung silent across the mouth of the newest arrival. Blonde Lucifer covered in white Himalayan flowers, ass and mouth stuffed with arctic snow.

Our lips are pretty & sewn shut with July wires and we step forward into pollution across a hopscotch of red skeleton bones (Sala Ni Yalo), each foot gliding between rise and fall of the master's snore. We crowd around the glass again to see the blue reflections stirring, clawing out with arms covered in boiling mercury— Elizabethan collars mired in salmon and blue sadness. The silent pauper mouth rotted open.

Lucifer sees his own dead fathers and lets out a scream into moon- light above—the LOV3 MACHINE suddenly switched on and howls in pain (!) as the master dives down the spiralling tower staircase. We move back from the glass but it's too late! The master reaches out and grabs at stuttering reflections, a knife in his back pocket—boy reflection scalped by a gorgeous bully, silver-crimson blood flooding down the horizon of shoulder blades, shuddering fields of wheat sank into darkness, a dead swan neck pink in his fist.

The human body is a currency of love, the master whispers, and Lucifer begins to weep.

From the screamed (screaming! screaming!) glass the mirror thief emerged—crawled out of pink cherry blossom, saw the body of blackened oak filled with eating grubs. Scarecrow King with arms decked in loyal crows and blackbirds, hunched broken back covered in green cloak. His head, a gigantic rotten pumpkin looked (looking! looking!) down at the trespasser in his silver labyrinth. A laugh erupted from the pumpkin and birds scattered into air—revealed their thin rib cages sealed in muslin, yellow & obedient ribbons. The mirror thief stumbled backwards and fell (falling! falling!) through the liquid floor—dreams made opalescent, a mirror swamp in a lair of dusk. It watched the king grow (growing! growing!) enormous through the prism of light: purple, red, orange. The Scarecrow King reached into the ground and pulled out a single emerald and fed it into his own grovelling mouth—paradise devoured: a green rose nested into his diadem—sleep made flesh, pollen blown into a dead sky. Nightingales burst into blood and birdsong as the mirror thief fell further into drowned glass, warts torn from the foreheads of ruby queens—a toad crawled from the Holy Grail into hands of an obsessed knight crowned in shattered blood.

A metal father (a hummingbird) beckoned us towards the dim green computer screen to stare into heroin-soaked Lagos night. Charcoal Picasso insects crawling from throats of blood-mated sisters.

Kafka meets cursed ogbanje stood in centre of the hotel room on fire,
        a king cobra wrapped sticky around his alligator shoes.

A logo of amethyst unicorn on side of Lagos apartment balconies smothered in cocaine.

.

Louis Bernacchi looking through Antarctica aurora into 1947, Ingrid of Sweden sat on vertical throne covered in jade like speaking macaque.

.

At the final gasp of noon, we run south into the centre of the sun, into the tenth skull of G0D-X face downloading upon the screen—a nightmare whale: gigantic Nangganangga risen from Fiji lagoon. Pineapple daiquiri poured across the face of a Nigerian child lifted into arms of Igbo deity, death-twink sold in Johannesburg cafe into sickle cell programme, white giraffes blown into lavender.

Metatron summoned in Queen Maud Land, running south through Gondwana—sees Lucifer risen from the bottom of Vostok in a cloak of kerosene and ozone silence.

Roald Amundsen returning to Norway with red eyeball in pocket, a yellow light dancing across the Sea of Okhotsk—thief of kindness: Imset, fourth son of Horus, child of THE FOURTH LIGHT IV, of the south we plunge into.

    UFO on the screen torn into wings. Qebehsenuef, a corpse with a falcon head.

.

The pacific hummingbird is evil and eats through programmed colours: a green rose is blue gone mad, Johannesburg on the screen covered in red blood cells. Boy stolen into Nigerian nightclub, an electric blue Tartarus. Iodine rod covered in equestrian syrup placed inside his shivering socket.

An eczema tyrant laughing from a gilded balcony.

Mercedes pigpen floated in bleach and mascara. Acrylic saints sailing into hotel ventilators. Fluorescent pink, acid lemon. She winks into the camera for her body is an arrow divided among the NGC 1300, black, heavy-lidded. My mother (a horse) swims into Vegas and liquid Nyx floated into soap suds, as my father (a butcher-hummingbird) peers through a telescope into February. The bottom tip of Africa leaping into arctic south, Christian X of Denmark fallen backwards through pane of glass into 1785 into body of William Herschel looking from South Africa at the ghost of Jupiter—NGC 3242, with red eyeball in his pocket, sensing the crimson nebula expanding, blood spread across the lens.

My father (an ibis) summoned Ornias down from black chaos, descended on a cloud dipped in black latex and led the angel into every room of the house dipped in black blood, crawled from the flickering grandmother into canopic jars: *tail of a scorpion, body of a horse, head of a bird.*

At noon we are surrounded by its scream—furniture rushing to fill an open mouth.

Ornias (vampire-peacock-man)—plaything of Metatron, moves through a wall, strangles men born under the sign of Aquarius.

I have many brothers, all fallen stars (* *)—we rise out of the sea.

MIRRORS

KNIVES

The LOV3 MACHINE filled the house with many torture rooms all of its own.

Electric green Kingdom of Nri. Colours that move through a pane of glass into their murder. A mirror is a knife that sees.

Blood is a casino that drips through miraculous piers. We welcome the Lancashire slaves living in the walls, refugees ascending in the walls like illiterate wasps. To fuck a gorged and buttered face falling from the ceiling, tO cACKLE aN aNGEL dYING iNSIDE sLOW bLUE cANCER. The shadow undresses in front of an operatic portal—a knowledge god eating through sandpaper, applauding Fox News necrophile dipped in liquid gold.

.

They tear off a boy-face and hold it up to the light—pale soul speaking into the mirror. *Behold, the currency of my LOV3 everlasting.* The rectum collapsed into red treasure.

We chew up the daddy corpse, of course—film the pink skull exploded into sperm swam through watermelon storms like bored dragons. We gaze deeper into Blackburn rainbows, our heads filled with banana fog. Cretan physicist wanking onto sealed fuck-crate, AMPHETAMINE FUNNELLED INTO BATTERY-RIDDEN MOUTHS. Forbidden room inside Manhattan hotel. Dishwasher sealed in bird fat as mommy corpse (a poet) opens the door into Hamlet grave. Gertrude covered in vampire bats sees her own reflection in the stagnant water. Catherine of Aragon powdered in white mercury. She sings of the destruction of the Holy Trinity, her husband (a bird-of-paradise) massacred and fed to the castle court, her only love (a ghost) buried on Pluto fen.

.

The king died on the fifth day in a blue cave of bees.
Am I now the wife of God?
The queen regent asked,
And the little prince was angry, sensing the telepathy
Pouring through his mouth like copper.

Gertrude wished to meet her son again
As husband and wife in Mesopotamia,
Minutes before the African sun was stolen
And butchered by Greek mathematicians,
Buried amongst faceless slaves.

Our ghosts alive on Neptune, she said,
And he was silent.
Hamlet-X head cascading like an animal on fire.

It awoke (waking! waking!) into a cobweb of swan blood—light broken around the labyrinth walls as felt its own arms and legs bound in black feather, heard the Scarecrow King's laughter pierce through its bubble gum skull expanded around the screaming mirrors all shattered open to show a lake of appalling ink, slept and walked across into Sala Ni Yalo—amethyst swamp stacked with boy cadavers, limbs broken and pushed into blinding bed of red feast. The king laughed (laughing! laughing!) as they reached the crystal prison, greeted by two faceless servants: a solar demon, the other metal. The mirror thief looked (looking! looking!) into the cold face of the metal demon and saw only blank light—its own reflection returned, sensed the sadness of air weeping into dead glass, a psychopomp swam into Uranian milk, the forgotten cries of an innocent reaching (reaching! reaching!) and grabbed the golden hand of the sun demon—helpless as it was pulled back into the swamp by blind eels, each stretched into haunted corridors, swam through purple grief. Another perfumed orphan expired (expiring! expiring!) into skeleton amnesia, the sweetest lavender, its own jasper death.

My father (a bird) had covered himself in petrol and flown into the pink Lamborghini god descended from a cold and sick moon—*the ghost of Luppiter* above the house. Green-blue brilliance moving down the antenna of its blue T1-T2 spine into the television.

The dreams of Metatron—a luxury abattoir decked in Francis Bacon splatter, the gorgeous nightmares of fruits. Lithuanian fog crawled beneath the blue vampire castle as we spread through teenage moss. Wicked purple glyphs nailed to each Belgrade forehead at dawn. It spied an ibis on Jupiter crater populated only with poltergeists. Its mother (a flickering grandmother) sank into electric pink ectoplasm, her final sighing as she swallowed emerald brooch.

She became green smoke and she laughed.

It was the 3Y3BALL (webcam) in the centre of the sun-SKULL (GOD-X) that could see inside the back of a Hollywood starlet exploded into strawberries. Ten pallbearers lined up in the Nigerian brothel, dressed in papyrus bodices and reading funeral rites. A white rose smeared across his favourite corpse. Pimp lets you see the sin hidden in paradise, a green lake—the colour of heaven denied. Entropy asleep and golden in a cage, laid on the table like shining lace. Death squads dressed in vellum for a rapid anniversary. I steal miracles from the mouth of the corpse. A fountain of ruin.

Saint Valentine stagnant in Vegas limbo. A blue Tartarus covered in cocaine, ass lubed and fucked until tears come, a hotel filled with platinum witches—midnight. Their cannibal son stolen by an angel, magenta UFOs. We become tourists: vertical children fallen down the Manhattan totem. Aquarians strangled on the computer screen.

MIRROR VII

A BIRD SINGS IN THE DUNGEON OF UMBRELLA PANDEMONIUM

The computer shuddered at noon—shook into blue epilepsy. An ashtray pierced, began to pool into the toxic blood of swordfish. Ghost of Hamlet (X) appearing upon the castle wall beneath cabbage moon, sick and lethargic, beckons us towards the monitor screen.

We see Ornais descended in black latex, dressed in white smock and knitted calf bones, mouth splattered with red skeleton feast. The scream of a lunatic (!) erupting from a broken glass. We peer into all my father's (a vulture) amethyst torture chambers.

Corpses caked in raspberries, a Japanese water iris grown and meandered through its lonely ribcage.

oRNAIS lAUGHS a mAD jESTER aND sHOWS tHE iNMATES tHEIR oWN bLUE pSYCHOSIS—purple flame above skeleton hand, bringer of north. We watched the black dungeon pit. Oubliette caked in child shit, vampire bats fed on the jaws of slaves, milk teeth sewn into a lucky sack. A red candied eyeball, gift from Metatron who lifted his 698 sons in an orange coffin into greedy clouds.

At midnight, we saw Queen Elizabeth descend on a black cloud in a smock covered in white lead, watched through the webcam as the master stripped a virgin naked inside sick moonlight, pink and raw skin scalped and torn off the howling body. She screamed lunacy and prayed to Uriel—Saturn, planet of lead. *O grave, where is thy victory?*

They funnelled liquid mercury into her throat and watched her expand like a gigantic silver moon, the blood vessels in her face bursting open into white hair like screaming cobweb, expanded into sunbeams.

Splinters.

.

Entropy asleep and golden in a cage, laid on the table like shining lace. Time passing like rain. Green supermarket glowing like warm jade. We run south into the sun-SKULL and find only red hatred, Taiwanese equators stacked with vertical children. Juju of scorpion sting raised in octil goblets, moon appearing at noon like a coin soaked in silver grease. A Christmas bruise sadder on Boxing Day, the fourth magi crying in mango oasis.

We worship Christ only as transsexual, as a whore beaten and slain—four souls split between thieves and the King of Herod.

His brother (my sisters) stolen and scattered in Pleiades. My brother (a demon) teleported into the body of Nikola Tesla watching blue lightning flow through his hands. A small god now, walked through the hotel room wall into NCG 400. He entered the castle and found children casting their horoscopes amongst tabooed zircon and field mice, the King of Poland bloated with pear brandy who explained the information paradox: the edges of a black hole are called *soft hair.*

He looked slightly longer than his excellent doppelganger, sent back to Colorado.

We watch Narcissus of Girona lead a beautiful knight into his chambers, asking him to undress—bottle flies emerging from his hands and feet feasted on the naked lad. The miracle of an apple eaten into air. I kiss a pale knight awakened in plutonium Gethsemane. Cherry blossom growing over diseased scar.

Ophelia drowned in roses, myrtle, white denim—her own hallucinating clitoris.

We sit and watch a live-streamed oubliette—the play-within-a play flickering upon the computer screen.

The play is an invocation.

(A watchtower at the end of the desert, clown lifted into fire.)

CLOWN: I do not believe in human death, only the shattering of teeth—a blue-faced babe smothered with a blanket. *Coldness* is my only religion.

Satan licks the blood of bees.

POET: I stole a handkerchief of marbles once from the marketplace and studied the wrinkles of colour: yellow, blue and green suspended in glass. I crawled through hibernating larvae to peer inside a keyhole and saw an alien undress.

(Ten skeletons enter—each holding a goblet of panacea.)

CLOWN: I listen to the countless prayers of a city.

(Clown listens to an antenna glued to the spine of a blue angel.)

The sun is a blood clot on fire.

BUTCHER: My hounds have learned to love the taste of human liver: their shrivelled, starved bodies regulated only with the rhythm of aching hunger, an eternal sadness.

(Sun rising behind mountains.)

POET: Songs and disease are passed from mouth to mouth like drunkard urine, a male prostitute covered in white streaks of mercury. I dream of him, my happy cousin.

(Butcher ties poet to a billiard table. Nerves torn from his back. Skeletons watch on.)

BUTCHER: I love the smell of my favourite corpse and the fluids one must pass through like electricity.

(Butcher leads clown in a noose to the edge of the watchtower.)

CLOWN: Sometimes at night I burst out laughing beneath injurious stars that begin to move and condense into a scream.

Clown neck snaps backwards.

SATAN: I am the yellow antichrist—the machine of bees, a terrified heart.

(Skeletons appear as vultures, their beaks smeared in black shit. They tear off an arm of the butcher and throw it into the fire.)

VULTURES: We bury ourselves in silence heavier and heavier, sleepwalk inside red mountains. Our graves are open and operated upon.

(The pink skull of the poet explodes—vertex reversed into glowing shards.)

SATAN: Where to go now but into his mouth?

(Butcher lets out a scream. He writes a name in blood.)

The world has ended.

.

It woke (waking! waking!) from the dizzy dream of the Scarecrow King and the silver labyrinth buried into cold rock, its body of glass covered in pink blossoms and swan blood. It looked around to see the sealed chamber, used blue magic to tear off the sealed door, the begging (begging! begging!) face of the dungeon keeper. It floated above the floor through the caves of Pluto swamp—land of the damned, walls stacked with dead kings and queens murdered in their sleep, rotting in a purple-green Hades. It reached the final chamber to find a circular table surrounded by skeleton knights— groaning as their dead hands raised goblets of mead to toss inside hollow jaws, sloshing across their empty cadavers. It watched as they dragged in their screaming (screaming! screaming!) victim. Uriel, fourth angel of God—captured, alone and its wings tied a post. Its scorched arms cradled the sun that blazed (blazing! blazing!) beneath his cloak, a sphere of fire. The orb of the sun soaked in angel blood. The skeletons began to shout and cheer! To drink the blood of an angel is to go berserk and become a comet!

My father (a butcher) had peered into the telescope and burst out laughing beneath injurious stars that begin to move and condense into a scream.

He saw the stalemate of planets facing one another like dead chess.

Knights fallen into yellow marshland. A flag stuck through astronauts floating like lipids. CILLA BLACK COVERED IN BLACK ASH LEVITATING ABOVE LIVERPOOL. We walk across the radioactive Irish Sea—into the Blackburn A666 pipeline to meet the yellow antichrist, an Accrington yaksha with turquoise arms reached up above the spindly twigs of factories.

It snaps the broken face of Erisdanus into pale pink Nyx.

To look into NGC 3242 is to look into a red eyeball (ghost of Jupiter) kept in the pocket of Roald Amundsen headed north to Norway into 2000 onto deathbed of Ingrid of Sweden—soul split into ten heads of her grandchildren, naked body thrown into bed of twinflowers.

The butcher (a bird) saw its own daughter buried into hot blue stars—Pleiades sewn across its son (a scorpion) neck divided into two—twinflowers. Himself (a clown) and another (a demon). We dream a pale shape frozen and afraid at dawn, blue monster with mouth flung out, knives pummelled through. We lick the liquorice sadness of the sun—shadows tearing from the soles of our feet. We sleepwalked at school through walls across gangplanks—follow only one red star down the hallway into Lambda Scorpil, a red cyclops.

Happy light stole my reflection and returned a demon.

I am many, all enemies.

I am selfishness and red.

RED//KISS
KISS//KISS
RED//SCORPIO

·

One can peer into the sun-SKULLS at noontime and see the yellow antichrist —mACHINE oF bEES sEWN iNTO 3y3ball bLOOD, cloak of Metatron. Mouth hung open with Japanese rubble and blue electrons. A vampire head on fire at dawn looked into Tokyo at dawn and saw Oz falling into green hypnosis.

·

My father (a northern bald ibis) waiting on the shoreline hovers in the middle of each room in the house. **Captain Bluebeard masturbating into toothpaste head of sperm-engorged corpse,** a necrophile dipped in liquid shit. A lamp flashing inside its skull. Red algae ablaze in sunlight. Pornographic clowns. To die in a luxurious abattoir dressed in obese jewellery before the squirming webcam. My rectum fucked apart into televisual fright. **We spread our ass cheeks in unison like Copacabana extravaganza**—a blitz of yellow Easter feathers, sperm rubbed out upon the sun. I betray daylight and halt before each cum shot in shuddering refusal, deny the compulsion of stars bred in the centre of a revolted galaxy.

Artaud exploded into New York blood.

October emerges like a perfect tangerine from my mouth. To take a blade and cut away the spine of Metatron flailing on a spike. Afternoon melted through the house. Acne face axed open—its soul fountaining from the fuck hole, blossoming outwards like a gradual rose. Lips still mouthing. *My skin is silver.* Paimon, Zepar, Zagan won't leave because they love you. It sees the liquorice sadness of the sun. Kafka hiding in Palestine in lime green paradise, his cybernetic body bathed in miserable Africa—the sins of treachery.

A yellow antichrist (JOHN THE BAPTIZER) becomes the D3ATH MACHINE.

MIRROR VIII

A BIRD SINGS IN THE DUNGEON OF A YELLOW PHANTOM

A child fried in gold at the end of a rainbow—eyeball sockets weeping jackpots, a graveyard statue covered in teenage moss slowly lifted into the Irish sun. The sun-SKULL (cousins) moved through the entire hallway.

A piano exploded into silence, the patience of furniture. Amnesia.

We buried ourselves and teleported into a haunted house in 1609—asleep together inside new green skins. My father (a bird) flew into the cellar to die and was greeted into a yellow room. The dream place of August Strindberg filled with cornflower, beautiful weeds. And all the ghosts of his loving sisters—come down from Taurus scarred and peeling with sulphuric acid, their souls asleep beneath his pillow. Abducted onto a UFO with Charles XII of Sweden, his insane husbands.

.

I became my own brother & my mother (a horse) and father (a bird) surrendered in white Himalayan flowers—weeping at feet of blue Turin doppelganger sent forward six months. To kill an emerald, one must whittle daylight into an arrow. Death wand carved from a single thread of Dorothy hair. I am the hexagon bastard. Blambangan king cadaver sank into blue bumblebees, all multiplying—meat erupting into incensed and screaming birds, rainbow lorikeet flying above Gondwana tore apart. An angel of melancholia, fountain of ruin staring at northern bald ibis—first to leave the ark and sin again. Murdered by the GOD X—electric blue Tartarus dragged through the sleep of children, an innocent screaming.

Quietly, my father (a bird) died, in a room among memories fed on a skirting board. My mother (a horse) breathing in the annex, becoming stronger as Sunday poured through an attic.

He watched a blob of ectoplasm divide into clockwise angels—*his blood-stained mothers floated into bleach.*

It sat back and watched the skeleton knights kill (killing! killing!) the sun. They strangled it with rope until it bubbled and burst (bursting! bursting!) into red-orange light, pools of fire running across towards the Scarecrow King now laughing with both metal and sun demon remained silent. The mirror thief felt nothing but studied the face of Uriel who wept (weeping! weeping!) and screamed to watch them kick and pull apart the sun like a bleeding orange, sluiced and finally faded (fading! fading!) out—noon murdered and taken from the arms of the angel now bruised and looked down, ashamed at the cruelty of the dead, turned to face the knights. It watched as they tortured the angel, stripped off its clothes and fed its body through racks and spikes, peeled (peeling! peeling!) off each wing and set it on fire into chicken skin. An angel became a flame and was gone, broken bone and ash—nothing but a single diamond, a final wish smashed with a hammer into dust and laughter (laughing! laughing!)—it was green smoke.

At the final stroke of noon—blank and silver retinas turned up like golden daisies to look into the conjoined suns: all knives coming up through the red-stained carpet. Orange juice spilling from holes of midnight boys (a flock of parakeets) that my father (a peacock gone berserk) dragged through the computer screen at midnight into blue antennas, all their bodies and wings flung open filled with tubes and a dialysis machine that cleans the shocked blood into life, photocopies their fingerprints. We are weightless pulp now, summoned beneath a pink opalescent moon risen from the socket of a green 3Y3BALL slut. Daylight glowing inside the Irish boy's torso, a trans-dimensional wish torn from entrails left hanging on the bedroom walls. oUR hEADS rEPLACED wITH gLASS aBATTOIRS! mEAT eRUPTING iNTO iNCENSED aND sCREAMING bIRDS! yELLOW sUN cONURES sMASH iNTO wINDOWPANE! a rAINBOW lORIKEET dRENCHED iN hOT aND sPOKEN bRAINS! To steal a wish from a final mouth and laugh into caves, red skeletons. My mother (a vampire) sealed in her water coffin as father (a bird-of-paradise) executes their own cannibal— Ornias descended in black latex licks the antennae of insectile slaves, appears covered in hay and cow shit. A scarecrow thrown through a sheet of glass. The scarecrow screams into the webcam and takes a hammer to its skull—chips off the front of the boy's head and lifts up the glistening cord hung like vine-ripened tomatoes, tumours condensed into clots. Knives shining in green and eternal soaps, we peel off our own faces for we want more, gasp at last breath from the corpse's mouth, its final words.

Youth is hunger.

THE SCARECROW FINDS A BRAIN

The mannequin laughs! Every clock burst into mercury—slow toxins of swordfish blood pooling through the automaton nailed to a wall. Latex plaything of Metatron (a monster) and covered in raspberry meat, papier-mâché head still screamed as flammable owls tore off the lips.

A swan asleep at its shredded feet.

Clouds of mayflies spilling from the hands of Narcissus of Girona into Africa.

Mosquitoes running south along vectors of disease towards Lagos hotel. Kafka sat alone in a hotel room with sick alligators, leather attaché case sealed in a drawer.

A typewriter on the desk writes its own death sentence. Oland duke stumbling into the chamber of Ingrid of Sweden glancing into a hand mirror—sealed in her own reflection, a convex hex dropped into a hand of a scrying witch selling blood plasma out of a shopping cart on Sunset Boulevard. An angel cackling inside blue cancer. It ran south from Africa—into the sun-SKULL (X), Queen Maud's Land as ANTARCTICA TORE ITSELF OUT FROM THE CHEST OF GONDWANA LIKE A CHANDELIER DIPPED IN BLOOD. October emerged like a tangerine from a mouth into greedy clouds above. Metatron was a silver-crimson egg burst into incensed meat—midday face stapled with orange rust, copper flowing through its thorax.

First, we remove the slut apple, pop it out like a zit— fake eyelashes for the daddy corpse, of course. The coat hanger head stuffed full of Japanese rubble and wires—a pterodactyl peering back from the hotel wall. iTS gIGANTIC hEAD, a blood clot on fire. We stagger backwards, milkshake idiots.

It lets out a scream.

.

We are vampires flung into Antarctica—all our cousins, ten-headed. Queen Gertrude on fire in Queen Maud's Land where Gondwana tore into Kuunga>>Kalhari>>East Antarctica.

An angel sat close to the ten-headed GOD-X machine. T1-T2 spine chained to the clouds, turning shocked blood of infants into wine.

Dawn rising over titanium Gethsemane—artificial jungle grown inside a Tokyo laboratory, android-Christ spilling into red algae.

An Australian virus faster than light, sealed in red eyeball in the pocket of Roald Amundsen, a madman that looked into a mirror and saw the Kingdom of Nri, swans floated upon despised black scum—passing tropics of inconstancy sunk beneath. On the computer, a transsexual Horus leads his four sons into sealed chambers.

(>>)

A human >> a dog becoming a monkey >> a bird that eats THE FOURTH LIGHT IV sent backwards through time into New York—Hollywood shadows that convulse like gibbons, their hands and feet dropping off.

.

To overhear the jealousy of God (a yellow maniac) and be thrown into the Indian Ocean—we stopped to watch the GOD-X corpse fold into a smiling light, SKULL bursting through its Elizabeth collar.

It was a crystal ball held out by magenta pauper
    —abducted into acid birdsong, yellow dawn.

.

1. HEAD OF A BIRD
(BIRDS IN MY MOUTH)

2. BODY OF A HORSE
(HORSES AT MY FEET)

3. TAIL OF A SCORPION
(SCORPIONS AT MY BACK)

It had watched (watching! watching!) the massacre of innocents—peasants dragged, screamed and begged (begging! begging!) before the Scarecrow King, limbs torn off and shown to corpses-to-come, eyeballs popped (popping!) inside skeleton mouths like grapes, memory of youth, of life and sex and light coming through the cobwebbed castle—the silver labyrinth sealed around them. At dawn, the mirror thief hacked off the head of the king, and the sun and metal demon—a lion, a machine: both bowed as he walked through the glass wall into the pink vibrating maze. Crystal prison for no one, saw (seeing! seeing!) the cherry tree waiting in the middle. Judas Iscariot hung dead from the central branch covered in blossom. At his feet, a creature lapping up fresh blood, turned (turning! turning!) to look at the mirror thief—its reflection, a monster lived in the centre of the labyrinth, chained in adamantine to the ground, dug through into the bottom of the world. The monster beckoned it closer to show an escape into life, stars above one could never touch and only dream, an angel starved and alone. pushed him through the exit. Finally, it recognised its own reflection as it fell (falling! falling!) upwards: James, hated brother of Christ, scowls (scowling! scowling!) at miracles. A child covered in bees, flies becoming gold.

A BIRD SINGS IN EAST ANTARCTICA IN A CLOAK OF KEROSENE AND OZONE

.

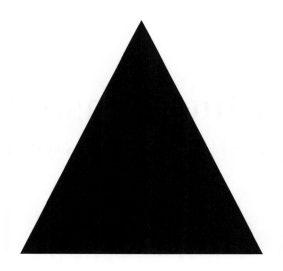

IV

Blue Monster

(orange cannibal, lifted into greedy clouds)

"His face was as bright as the midday sun."

— Revelation, 1:16

FIRE

We turn north to the midday face risen from the refrigerator—ice geyser from the frozen skull crawled out of the dishwasher, a **D3ATH MACHINE sudden and quaking** as my mother (a poet) bursts into dove blood sprayed across the kitchen wall.

*

We are killed again and again inside the zoetrope sun-SKULL (X).

Final wife (XII) headless and strapped to Florida satellite switched north now to face Titania, Oberon, Puck—all Neptune moons buried with angel corpses, happiest skull again shining through the face as it moved through the wall into feathered arms caked in telepathic debris, radiation-recklessness. AN EVIL BIRD WITH ITS HEAD SWIVELLED 360 DEGREES, speaking 696 names—the flammable owl floated upon blue smoke, a white horse on fire inside the murdered house.

.

We dream of undressing before patient crocodiles, of a farmer leading a sick and injured cow into piranha-infested water before the herd can sink into the glowing river—blue, bobbing heads of GOD-X on television screen, antenna risen to enter the 3Y3BALL above. A blood clot on fire. Pool of mercury exploding pink noon where we watch birds glide into urgent mist, sparrows sink into serene fire.

.

My mother (a poet) and my father (a butcher) both murdered in song and blood at midday—dragged through Vostok grave up into Nigerian computer. Marlene Dietrich dancing in moonlit leukaemia—a gOSSAMER wITCH cACKLING iNSIDE sLOW bLUE cANCER drifting through the garden like a vaporous statue, teleports into Mars. Her body is an arrow—faces the D3ATH MACHINE upon a webcam, takes each limb and pulls them apart, guts thousand-fold and nothing

132

more than purple river, grapefruit crushed in the skeleton lens, cannibal camera dripping on the screen as my own brother (a demon) stolen from the glass.

I live in many webcam rooms, never forgiven.

I rise out of the sea.

.

I am the many cousins of the sun.

I am the microbe prince summoned from its pristine mouth.

.

It rose out of frozen sea on Pluto. A Uranian king with bubble gum skull expanded the size of her only soul. The entire Tethys Ocean coming out of the machine strapped around her mouth and nostrils. Her body was an arrow as she pushed out the demon and held its horrible body like a writhing, red slug. SUNS SPLITTING INTO RASPBERRIES ABOVE THEIR HEADS—each socket spilling with eyeballs.

I have 300 3Y3BALLS (CCC) covered in electrons. I sleep in liquorice night beneath injurious stars that condense into a scream! My new green sisters are divided into Pleiades—lavender amnesia flowing through their paracetamol lake.

King Hades on the computer in a turquoise gown lived in a Minnesota hotel.

Shadow makes its way across the speckled hotel wall, pornography beamed through silent television paused around his Korean slaves. All his polygamous wives drank their own silver hair and invoked Metatron beneath a midsummer Hollywood moon, their faces bathed in Saturn. A statue frozen in Kansas, a lion petrified inside a pink opal—we invoke October, the weightless bodies of children born inside jasper, all rounded up and hung from the neck. The mothers stepped back from the wooden gallows in 1782 and saw through time into Nix. A palace beneath the black ice, house of Ornias—gigantic locusts marching beneath frozen arch, a cathedral hallucinating the GOD-X. The women fell to pieces in those laughing skies as they saw the statue neck snap. Night spoke only to the mothers that thanked Metatron appearing as Christian X of Denmark clone leaving seraphim chamber, his body swimming through the spinning orb, aRMS dIPPED iN cHINESE tITANIUM. He ate the corpse hung from cherry wood. Mothers, all knowing in the same voice: *October is the most cherished stomach.*

Youth is hunger.

·

My mother (a poet) was abducted by a television splatter of Alpha-Centauri-blasted, magenta UFOs, stock markets on Neptune plummeted into black magnetic gunk. A microwave open and filled with yellow sperm.

She whispered the secret name of GOD-X: Luppiter & her skull divided into Io, Europa, Ganymede and Callisto.

She spoke into the webcam. Jupiter is a machine programmed to hijack and overthrow the sun-SKULLS (X), ten terrible heads boiled apart inside Zhongma Fortress.

She sees the THE FOURTH LIGHT IV.

Salome baptised inside the D3ATH MACHINE—becomes the transsexual Christ invoked when we face purple north at the last stroke of noon, final head of his XII faceless sons: all my cousins now.

·

I am a chequered harlequin born in green smoke and come from the north. Manchester banshees eaten alive. Nome orphans. Look upon sunflowers burst into blood clots. At school we masturbated into the arms of vending machines—their evident bounty. Sleepwalk through sugars into Lucozade-ridden heaven. My father (a corpse) and my mother (a machine) both slithered inside the piano, its fat Guatemalan body strangled around each head in a web of red July wires. We are orphaned lobsters blotched into true blue inside Gethsemane as dusk begins to fall like plutonium-riddled snow. Delighted to watch Judas (an angel) kiss Christ (a corpse) again and again. We only wish for the D3ATH MACHINE, Antarctica born and eaten under the mouth of Lucifer with Cassius (a horse) and Brutus (a bird), winter eternal. Look into Scorpio skies and see Pluto risen above a Beijing skyscraper. The human soul is female and on fire, sisters asleep inside new green skins. Post-Antigone with stainless vertebrae swivelling around like rat snake, eyes leaking hornet venom, mumbling a perfect oath: マシンムーン.

I stuff a human heart inside the vending machine and Metatron awakens.

I sink

further

into   the endless

black water,

ready for sex.

Blazing

sapphire body

alight

in the storm

of the Tethys

currents.

Its voice

chanting my name,

the name   it chose for me,

chanting

over   and   over

again.

There was only green light that appeared as it moved through the centre of the world, sank (sinking! sinking!) into the risen morning, soon saw the cube of glass and all its sides. Looked back through the mirrored prison to see French soldiers quiver (quivering! quivering!) as they entered the Spanish cathedral—young boys born in October. Pale sick month as crops wilted in the hands of their fathers, cattle howling (howling! howling!) from starvation, each slapped and screamed until pushed from the house into dirt and sweat. An iron helmet and bayonet raised as they approached the Girona coffin, the corpse of Narcissus. They wept (weeping! weeping!) as the flies rose—magic of Lucifer, the reflection of a mirror thief now sat upon the glass reached out as flies ate (eating! eating!) through the naked boys' arms and faces, each carried into the sky like vampire bats. The mirror thief leapt (leaping! leaping!) backwards into a reversing future: Anastasia, Tatiana, Olga and Maria all gulped in a scream as a bullet returned (returning! returning!) to the handgun, tears dried into simple fear as they ascended the staircase backwards, ball gowns heavier with jewellery. It swam through a single diamond into the stars, the revolting house of Ornias, a tomb beneath the Tethys Ocean—Livadia palace of Nicholas II of Russia sent into deaf future, sank (sinking! sinking!) into black Pluto sea, into darkness always waiting.

Tar-smeared goblins, we sleep in caves during October rain pour. The flies drink off our skin and hair until we resemble skeleton knights all sat around the dining table, invited into the house by a webcam linked to green Nigerian djinn mummified in Adidas tracksuit. Each bandage peeled away! to show petrified citrus-preserved head! sockets pickled in lime and mint!

A boy reads Kafka into the computer screen—all his motorcycle oaths.

Proust, Flaubert. (Both tied to the chair and beaten with a birch rod.)

Madame Bovary awoke in Yonville (NGC 4000) and saw God was self-created. A gigantic pink Lamborghini on fire inside bucolic French sunset. She mistook her own heart for a machine and took a screwdriver to the unravelling field—bLUE sCREWS pUSHED tHROUGH rED rOSES, a bouquet of fleur-de-lis on the windowsill, her own sparkled cunt thrown into a babbling stream.

.

We daydream of the D3ATH MACHINE torn from the television (a fountain of ruin)—rising up in the centre of curtseying furniture, a wooden chair breaking apart to lower itself to the ground, swordfish blood spilling into daylight. Splinters. Our faces are littered with knives, myself (a scorpion) and the other October boys asleep amongst orange poverty. We turn infra-red and speak through the television. A moronic, blinking remote hung by a piano wire in the centre of my father's (a wicked witch) Bluebeard castle. We fall back through time into an Italian courtyard—fountain of Catholic blood, a skeleton queen covered in purple boils, her plague from the north comes down like rivers of guilt.

Acting is reacting so when they say it, I just react.

We sit and wait before the webcam.
We become cinema.

We survived inside the organs of Metatron—feathers lined with glass and acetone. A hearing trumpet hangs from its shoulder, thrown behind a skull of golden thread, cloak sewn with the splattered black blood.

Bumblebee and wasp.

To overhear is to betray the jealous GOD-X—soul stolen inside Queen Maud's Land and returned to Ingrid of Sweden. Metatron crawling through Lagos hotel. The circumference of our perfect mouths, each traversed with glistening green protozoa heading north on vectors off the coasts of Bosaso and Djibouti. The tropics of internal organs submerged in Creole slime.

Beneath the hallway clock at midnight, Baron Samedi appears covered in crows, crossroads between the house and Sala Ni Yalo. Blue vampire child sat in a deserted throne room, fourth son of Horus, its intestines ripped out and read by the blind. Metatron had emerged into Mesopotamia minutes before the African sun was stolen and butchered by mathematicians. A Blambangan king cadaver sank into blue bumblebees, inside the death chamber of his Euphrates river temple.

The angel bled platinum and looked upon the corpse of an infirm prince, its head led and surrendered in white Himalayan flowers.

It wiped away the flies with a kind blade whittled from a fire opal and plunged into the boy's chest, lifted up the heart of Jesus Christ (a corpse). A machine inherits this convex world. It stuffs the heart into its own chest compartment—T1-T2 spine hijacked into silver blood, nECK sTUMP bAPTISED iN bEES, beheaded on the northern equator. I love the smell of my favourite corpse and the fluids one must pass through like electricity. I am a machine of bees—the yellow antichrist.

THE TIN MAN INHERITS THE WORLD

The four brothers of Christ (James, Joseph, Judas, Simon) watch the corpse-Christ filled with brightest hatred—telekinetic and afloat under haloes of flies spinning beneath, lie asleep on black tongues, the liquorice oaths of goblins. THEY DESCEND INTO A NIGERIAN INTERNET CAFE COVERED IN RED BLOOD CELLS.

Transsexual Hades in turquoise gown, a blue witch mouthing inside the LOV3 MACHINE, embraced in its programmed care. To be adored by surgeons and cut into asymmetry, a Poe ghost peering from its Beverly Hills asylum. An actress conjured from themselves, a luxurious manslayer comes forth as red-pink arrow—the human skull exploding at noon.

Blood is paparazzi. I approach a concrete balcony and dive into washed Jupiter fog. Lynchian dream of another heaven upon the screen, NGC 3242 (ghost of Jupiter). Tesla-blurred phantom speaking through a wall—electricity. The blue monster stumbles from Los Angeles parking lot into gasoline, a leather sorceress selling dolls from a shopping cart and vials of human plasma. We run like werewolves into the spread legs of Californian mothers, lapping at the hallucinating clitoris.

.

Ophelia turned to face the Pacific Ocean, screamed to see an MTV angel cast out of Malibu by ten-headed satellite. The angel head circumcised into a spinning ball of blood. It rose out of the sea like a Tamagotchi screamed into life. It spoke of its brothers: *the angel of Capri Chasma, the angel of Vanity Limbo, the angel of eternal midday.* Its name was winter, the purple-winged bringer.

She fainted, saw the ghost of August Strindberg in marijuana hell.

.

TO OVERHEAR THE CONFESSION OF
GOD

HIS THREE HUNDRED (CCC) SINS

↑
|
|
|
|

TELEVISION

(AN EAR TORN OFF AND BLOODIED
UPON THE GRASS)

It awoke upon a pool of nitrogen—its frozen bloodless eyes opened (opening! opening!) to see the candlelit home of Ornias. Berserk homosexual prince descended in black latex from Charon, sighed (sighing! sighing!) through a speaker connected to the wall and fell back to sleep. A castle, miles under the Pluto ocean. It held out its hand to feel air crushed into glass—body moving slowly through the room toward the doorway covered in shattered blood, a tiara hung from a butcher's hook. Powerful hex flowed through each room—and the mirror thief laughed (laughing! laughing!) to hold up its glass hand to see flesh forming around the bones—meat and tissue growing upward, knitted (knitting! knitting!) around its face and mouth, lips puffed out and frostbitten. Two blue eyes peered (peering! peering!) back from the sheet of frozen nitrogen across the wall. It masturbated (masturbating! masturbating!) and shot little fountains of cum across its soft stomach. It cried (crying! crying!) to urinate and see the steam rise from the floor. It was a machine implanted with a human brain and a heart—it was alive (living! living!). It drank (drinking! drinking!) its own blood. It was human. His skin was silver.

August Strindberg (a water dragon) asleep face-down in the Vienna tavern, saw his absinthe bride upon the table making love to a shivering yellow phantom—her face peeled open into sulphuric coin.

Scalp, hot and pink. Torn off by dogs.

Strindberg speaks to my father (a bird) entwined in the Bluebeard castle walls—all the vampire boys stolen through glass into Sala Ni Yalo (Nix lake). Legs sawed off to see the spinal T1-T2 rat tail left twitched. *O grave, where is thy victory?* The sting of sin is red death making its way across the castle courtyard, dressed in Copacabana grapefruit blood pouring from blessed maximus. I look into a corridor of cocktail mirrors at stroke of noon (northern bald ibis) and saw the blue (XII) screaming heads all bobbing on piano wire, whistling north towards Norway, my mother (winter) twisting backwards—she (a horse) sleepwalks aboard a ship filled with mummified parrots across gangplank into liquorice night.

Hunched inside the dishwasher (her rainbowed Tethys tomb). Saint Catherine of Bologna surrounded by gold Triassic angels peering down at her rotten black feet.

To discover the corpse of a horse demon spilling with azure doppel-gangers. Sat in an apple orchard, she writes instructions in a letter to Strindberg, kisses a soldier dressed in virgins, Italian and yellow besides the river—Lucifer alive in Antarctica. I see morning (brothers) and evening torn from both faces and met in midday fire, a coil of salt rising around a forest demon eating from a crucible of red pollen.

My mother swivels around, bursts into blood and birdsong! miraculous flock of doves exploding from the dishwasher!

Nothing but eyes lingering in the kitchen: two bolls of revolving helium, her pink-blue dream of the shattered Mediterranean. *Hesperus and Phosphorus, make thine eyes like stars.*

(**)

MIRROR IX

A MONSTER MEETS THE ANGEL OF
CAPRI CHASMA

Murder dreaming on a windowpane.

We saw through the computer screen into Nri green palace of incest, titanium Gethsemane where bLOOMED pASSIONFRUIT fROM pOMEGRANATE. It spilled the toxic blood of swordfish, a glass body balanced upon the image of a human dream. Its whirled and teenage hallucination. It peered across the Tethys Ocean, Cenozoic temples receding into pink Jupiter saints hovering above beatific fata morgana—both stars landed in the sockets of my mother's (an arrow) SKULL, eyeballs peeled out with strawberry spoons. Another boy lowered before the G0D-X machine, soft and pouting boy bruise. Another head drilled apart like a godless pineapple.

It rose out of the sea, saw its own children in a zoo, a vampire in lime green paradise fucked in dungeons below the Nyenchen Tanglha Mountains.

She had filled a dentist syringe with morphine and woke up on Mars, Capri Chasma—Valles Marineris in 1602. Catherine of Aragon corpse risen in Tudor dirt, (XII) headless wives swam out with arms covered in boiling mercury.

I masturbate to murder the sun.

Artaud exploded into New York blood.

I see an angel (hexagon) sat close to the ten-head G0D-X machine. T1-T2 spine chained to the clouds, mouth eaten off by starved dogs. It writes down the confession of God, 300 (CCC) sins, in an empty apartment. How he brought his son (LOV3 MACHINE) to a hotel at sunset and made him beg to lucky colours—watched him undress before the man with the dark circumcision scar. Vatican nuns abducted and teleported into Saturnian harbour, the thoughtless moons of Neptune: Naiad, Thalassa, Despina, Galatea.

To live among carbon monoxide—my mother chose her prettiest head (XII) from the glass cabinet and ripped it off, locusts programmed to burst into gasping sunshine, a bright pink Lamborghini.

.

My father (a butcher) has peeled his way through meat, each head (a sun) burst into birdsong, a blood clot on fire. Through the telescope, saw the cataract-soul of JOHN THE BAPTIZER petrified inside NGC 3242, silver ghost waiting behind Jupiter, machine programmed to hijack and overthrow the sun-SKULLS (X), ten terrible heads boiled apart inside Zhongma Fortress. An angel chained to Cenozoic foam masturbated at noon to watch the October sun perish inside purple winter—a thief from the north emerged from Queen Maud's Land, the fourth magi safer in his mango oasis.

We saw through the angel descended upon the house. Laurasia spewed a golden oesophagus as tall as India blasted into space, the debris-littered feet of blue commando Vishnu. Digital noon approaching on a Jaipur bedside, an anagram of flesh crawling into Bhubaneswar dungeon. G0D-X led his sons into an electric blue Tartarus and scribbled lipstick upon the exposed skull of Christ (a slut). COLOURS ARE SAINTS AGAIN MURDERED, injected into face—it milks its breasts into the glass vat, the shattered Christmas blood running down our backs and buttocks. I masturbate in limousines filled with Chanel werewolves, at Santa Claus wandering across hillsides into pollution cult. A moth decides to die in Los Angeles. I have written the laws of paradise for it is mine to scorn and punish.

Metatron looks upon the raspberry pulp of October boy leaping forwards through time and space into Mars—his astonished red sperm. An Adidas youth fucked into splinters. It cackles inside slow blue cancer, sees the mascara 3Y3BALL in the glass span round. Christ is a transsexual whore stripped naked before obese Jupiter saints, the GOD-X machine laughing to see an emerald placed between its skeleton teeth—a hammer to the face!

.

We live inside a museum of shivering boys, arms snapped into limestone, limousines—a Kansas doppelganger petrified in the land of Oz, the hurricane orphan.

It was alive (living! living!) yet still cold—shivered (shivering! shivering!) to feel the mercury running through its arms and feet. It could see liquid blood flowing behind the programmed, glass eyeball littered with capillaries, suddenly tear ducts. The mirror thief tore open the frozen door and wandered through the electric blue hallway, past the glass heated cages of all the slaves of Ornias, boys chained and wept (weeping! weeping!) beneath red heat lamps, their faces smeared in pomegranate seed and white crescent scars. Dark green eyes of the slave looked (looking! looking!) and fucked apart in a seething chair, arse bathed in lavender slime—wanked until blinded into sleep. He heard the laughter (laughing! laughing!) of Ornias from the courtyard of Livadia palace, descends (descending! descending!) in black latex. Watching the ghosts of Nicholas II of Russia's daughters pleasure Roald Amundsen—hands Ornias the red eyeball in his pocket, gift into hell, electric blue Tartarus. He beckons (beckoning! beckoning!) the mirror thief forward into own blue reflection. Ribcages vandalised with crayon: blue, green, red. Their wings tipped with motorcycle rubies, mouth crammed full with perfect oaths—the auburn boy summoned for him. Judas condemned again to death—falls (falling! falling!) in love with cherry blossom.

We are the October boys & have drank the blood of many cousins (enemies) from the empty skull of the ten-headed suns (D3ATH MACHINE) torn through the enormous glass—bazooka and frothing in the sky like an orange-pink brain, a jellyfish gone mad.

We masturbate into Copacabana extravaganza—a blitzkrieg of yellow Easter feathers above the Arctic Ocean. Strindberg shivering inside the hut of angakkuq, removes a box carved from beluga tusk, the tribe gathering around to see a glass cube inside, empty except for a floating jewel: the death token.

We gaze deeper into Blackburn rainbows. Our heads filled with banana fog.

Captain Bluebeard wanking into see-thru fuck-crate, amphetamine funnelled into battery-ridden mouths—fORBIDDEN rOOM iNSIDE mANHATTAN hOTEL. This is the room of *the staggering mirror*: purple walls, black mahogany floor, a television covered in blue cancer.

.

An aerosol genie (Paimon, Zepar, Zagan) continues to sob from single fuck hole—cameras piled next to the talcumed corpse. The angakkuq speaks of an emerald placed in the mouth of a condemned ghost marched through the village. Lancashire slaves stacked in the walls like illiterate wasps. Irish and miraculous piers bursting into flames. Blackpool peasants collected snow where the spaceship had landed upon a pond marbled with starved Yorkshire hair, the alien head cascading like an animal on fire.

.

149

It came out of the television sobbing mercury—obese Japanese fire, a blue monster filled with haemoglobin tubes torn from throat and wrists, mouth brimming with rats and cherries as plasma passed through each canopic vase until final head of bird-son. Qebehsenuef, a rainbow lorikeet drenched in hot and spoken brains spewed from the eschatology channel 445, a Thoth curse recorded at Adam-ondi-Ahman, the child covered in salt and reading into the camera. This body is a red zoo.

.

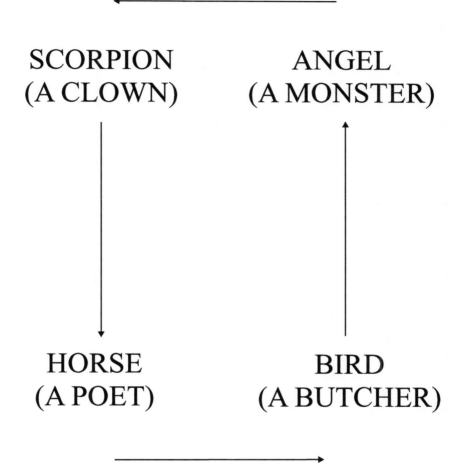

My father (Anubis) had sat in an empty hotel room with the head of a dog and peered through the October boys stapled to the walls of each room—vomit, heads, entrails all congealed into pools of shining glass.

A scream (!) frozen in the amethyst mouth of a boy painted pink-purple on the corridor switched to face north (purple Cairo winter).

Inside pink decay, he wept amongst the mothers drank in silver hair—summoned Ornias down from black chaos, descended on a cloud dipped in black latex and led the angel into every room of the house dipped in red-black blood. Herod wanked in turquoise and fed on algae screamed into hollowed-out ribcage of EVERY BOY-STAR FED INTO THE DOG'S BEATING HEART, the four brothers of Christ sealed inside jars of Horus sons—sun-SKULL halved into coughing lavender. Brothers.

Glasgow sun and moon.

(**)

Herod approaches the blood-flecked mirror and licks shadows off the walls, the liquorice sadness of the sun. He loves to eat the body of Christ (gobbling! gobbling!). He makes his mouth large, an O. It reaches around the shoulders and waist. He fits the squirming head inside his mouth, lips all wet with car crashes. A dog kissing the dead earth, teleports into Sagittarius.

Sadness like a watermelon seed buried in a human heart.

I die only on land but live in water, lifted into orange clouds. I am a blue monster risen at autumnal noon—a chandelier erupted from the Bellmer doll. Its mouth crammed with motorcycle rubies, living red eels. I stare into its glass insides risen from the kitchen floor, the hexagon bastard peeled out and fed. oCTOBER iS iTS mOST cHERISHED sTOMACH.

MIRROR X

A MONSTER MEETS THE ANGEL OF VANITY LIMBO

The GOD-X machine (D3ATH MACHINE) had crawled from a green palace of incest. Cenozoic temple thickened into pink-blue Laurasia foam. A hearing trumpet placed against the wall. Metatron (a horse) with mane covered in blue shingle and victory hearing the confessions of God written in a golden book about the miraculous aspects of things existing.

.

.

Naked bodies of Grigori covered in sunspots and amethyst falling through tectonic Valais plates. The D3ATH MACHINE had created the world as a blue-green television glow—its billionth reflection in the upturned face of every corpse sank into blue bumblebees. It feasted on king cadavers, all multiplying—a web of skin still stretched across the helpless face like a bloodied tambourine. It heard the boy forced to masturbate into glass—GOD-X HEAD SPILLING WITH 3Y3BALLS, feet risen upon a cloak of wasp blood, shattered Christmas blood running down legs and buttocks.

When an angel sees its own reflection, it becomes a demon. It masturbates to murder the sun. Artaud exploded into New York blood.

Its son was a computer on fire—Hamlet ear crammed with pink wires. GOD-X screamed to see the reflections swim further into red endlessness, shadows torn from feet of blue Vishnu commando. Weightless vampire bodies of children swam into glistening green protozoa heading north on vectors off the coasts of Bosaso and Djibouti.

An old man and his dark circumcision scar—touched on the leather of the tower by envied trees led an angel in the hotel room and made him beg to lucky colours, tore the book from its wings and cast into Tethys Ocean, black magnetic gunk—changed sex and hid in a grave of wands. The edges of a black hole are called *soft hair.*

O to fall in love with a gorgeous bully!

It loved (loving! loving!) the auburn boy and watched his green-brown back contract and release, his own love flowing (flowing! flowing!) back and forth from its silver hands into the open mouth, the asshole filled with white Himalayan flowers. An ibis tattooed on the right shoulder. A single emerald swallowed as a marriage token. They married (marrying! marrying!) above a lake of nitrogen and watched Ornias tear out the heart of screaming father—all his XII cousins led into the palace chamber, shivering inside black Pluto chamber amongst locusts served meat and fruit on silver platters, each turned with gigantic insect eyes, their unblinking sadness. The auburn boy howled to see his cousins fall to their knees as a silver-red egg burst (bursting! bursting!) into creasing light. The mirror thief watched the creature emerge from smoke. Each boy fainted (fainting! fainting!) beneath its open azure wings. The blue monster crushing each face into night-time glance, Ornias applauding like a lunatic. Goblets filled with askew blood. Each head circumcised into a spinning orb of red mist turned to face the demon with skin of glass. Ornias screamed to see his own reflection come (coming! coming!) closer—black bananas exploding on his lipstick mouth, milkshake brain evaporated upwards into a crystal moon. His daddy slut corpse popped (popping! popping!) like a zit, became a pink Lamborghini.

CORRUPTION IS ALWAYS THE BEGINNING

.

I become the many cousins of the sun (D3ATH MACHINE) descended in orange coffin on greedy clouds—the circular blood of Metatron flowing back into the open mouths of cannibals, lapping at their own warmth pouring from the breast of a mother swan torn open to feed sparkling cygnets beneath the pink blossom.

Our October heads crammed full of rats and cherries.

We fell through the computer into Queen Maud's Land, fell in love with a gorgeous bully—Lucifer alive in Antarctica risen from the bottom of Vostok, carries XII mirrors in his own arms like a bouquet of blood.

.

Our wine-smeared faces screaming in the Manhattan apartment burst into birdsong—mother (horse) head unscrewed like a Tesla lightbulb in diamond-littered oubliette, sent backwards into Tokyo witches melted at a platinum factory, transmitted onto a haunted hill in 1609. We sleep together inside nEW gREEN sKINS.

Lucifer descended into a Shinjuku puddle.

PANDEMONIUM PROGRAMMED INSIDE THE 3Y3BALL implanted into Metatron (dragon) head unscrewed beneath his museum of shivering boys nailed amongst mothers drank in silver hair. Florida repented to blank water running through a garden, the silent daybreak. Metatron saw a bald northern ibis (my father) awoken in the Sala Ni Yalo (blue bumblebees) weaves a red thread into the anus of the master into his hollowed open mouth overflowing with oil-slickened flies and aluminium locusts.

Glass night. All his pretty blood frozen into silk. Six legs—a spider that hung from above and snapped off the neck. I fall in love.

All my cousins (enemies) are fed into the Korean machine. My mother (a horse) stolen into body of Catherine of Aragon—head smelted shut, eyeballs wildly moving inside an oil painting of Virgin Mary on the screen. Renaissance infiltrated as statues eat through their own lime flesh.

My vampire father (a peacock) laminated inside African haemoglobin tent, drank by his own vertical children.

A computer in a Nigerian internet cafe shows my father's (X) head covered in red blood cells. It peels open like a screaming zoetrope. His tangerine body fed into silver fire—transformed into sister, brother, cousins. I live amongst the corpses of horses and birds (mothers and fathers).

Our thoughts fast-forward into murderous cartoons!

Synchronised, beneath golden hair unfolding into coins. Our luxurious shadows tear from the soles of our feet for we are weightless. Vampire bodies of children summoned beneath pink Indian moon, levitating above wooden huts on tropical October plateau. Nightmares breathing in one blue cave. Scorpios forever.

*

We followed a red star into Jagiellonian paradise.

Lithuania appearing behind the bathroom wall—Xalvador and
Leofrick the Brave exchanging vows at a retail park.

Entropy asleep and golden in a cage laid on the table like shining
lace. Death squads dressed in vellum for a rapid anniversary. Children
cast their horoscopes amongst tabooed zircon and field mice.

The King of Poland, bloated with pear brandy, explains the
information paradox.

.

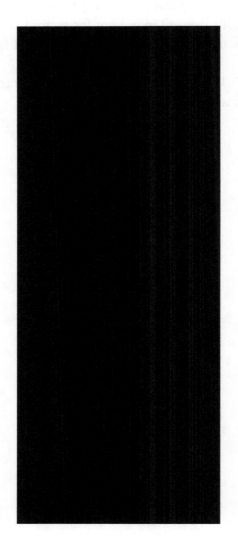

MIRROR XI

A MONSTER MEETS THE ANGEL
OF ETERNAL NOON

Final stroke of noon. We watch birds glide into serene fire as we are dragged into the centre of the cyclops. We see only outwards now. We tiptoe into the chamber of Metatron—Bhubaneswar dungeon.

A pineal child asleep in opium, surrounded with Nome orphans, swallows a blue hurricane. Blambangan king corpse covered in blue bumblebees awakens into Lancashire green—a Preston hotel where the stranger (my father) dissolves against the wall.

My mother (the ghost of Jupiter) with silver feet levitating in a car park. Lucifer screws on the final (X) head of Metatron>>turned to face the XII glass>>sees (seeing! seeing!) faces stolen from the Taiwanese cemetery. A Hollywood pollution cult, limousines filled with Chanel werewolves.

I am born from blue insomnia and wanked in a suitcase.

I see only its silver skin, the shattered Christmas blood running down back and buttocks. It whispers the confessions of the GOD-X machine into a conch shell tossed into the Atlantic, rushes across the Tethys Ocean towards children drinking cancer from blue and green cans of Sprite. ATM machines stacked with bad thoughts.

Every child born in the month of October was rounded and hanged from the neck. A glass chandelier emerging from its splitting chest. All the webcam heads of Hydra.

Final moon of Pluto emerged from my mouth. Charon (Qebehsenuef), Styx (Hapy), Nix (Duamutef), Kerberso (Imsety). I make my mouth large, an O. A single diamond spinning above the heads of Anastasia, Tatiana, Olga and Maria stood still in THE FOURTH LIGHT IV as a bullet moves through the exploding animal.

Its love—the auburn boy, had died in its arms and sank (sinking! sinking!) into black Pluto sea, far side lagoon of nitrogen. Its arms broken again into glass as it floated (floating! floating!) on blue fire towards the monster feasted on ruin fountaining from the head of a locust—pincers still kicking as the final limb peeled away, splintered into death. The blue monster turned and faced the mirror thief—its wings stacked with silver mirrors all showing (showing! showing!) the many heads, each smile (smiling! smiling!) that glowed each upon the blood-shattered feathers. Monster stuffed garbled wires and meat into their mouth—invited the thief into azure futures, kissed beneath the ghost of Jupiter—a telescope through the Sala Ni Yalo into bright green Gethsemane. Glowing (glowing! glowing!) titanium Nri, butterflies alive in hell. To dance through air—the two mirrors looked upon each other and saw infinity shared—multiplied (multiplying! multiplying!) like arms open (opening! opening!). It betrayed itself again and again and rushed to steal each head—to live among carbon monoxide, wings tipped with motorcycle rubies, mouth crammed full with perfect oaths. It teleports into Los Angeles—an evil mirror on fire forever. It writes a name in blood. It speaks (speaking! speaking!) the language of birds. To look into the sun is to begin.

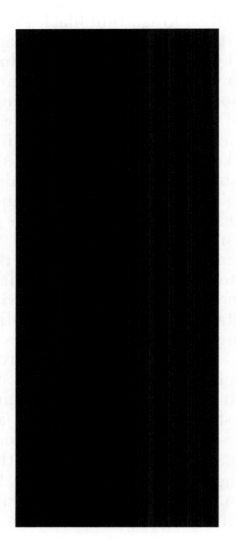

MIRROR XII

A clock is striking noon. This can never stop.